Farm Girl

Farm Girl

(Mostly) Minnesota Editions

Hannah-
Enjoy the
book!

Joyce Pearson

By
Joyce Pearson

Photo, front cover: The childhood home of the author
Photo, back cover: The author with her grandchildren and great-granddaughter

This is a work of fiction. Names, characters, places and incidents either are the product of the author's imagination or are used fictitiously.

To order copies of other books endorsed by the author, *We Just Shoveled Two Feet of Partly Cloudy, A Winter Sabbatical, and From Peace Corps with Love,* please contact: (Mostly) Minnesota Editions; 2307 Gibley Park; Toledo, Ohio, 43617; *jpatber2@ utnet.utoledo.edu*

This book was printed in the United States of America.

To order additional copies of this book, contact:
Xlibris Corporation
1-888-795-4274
www.Xlibris.com
Orders@Xlibris.com
79412

I have dreamed of writing a book for many years and have started hundreds of times, only to throw away each sheet of paper. Throughout these years, the theme and name of my book has remained the same. *Farm Girl* is a dream that has, at last, come true.

—Joyce Pearson
August 1, 2010

Acknowledgements and Dedication

I want to thank my sister, Judy Patberg, for editing my book and for encouraging me to believe in myself.

I have written this book in honor of my immediate and extended families, and it is to them that I dedicate *Farm Girl*.

Introduction

"Another day, another dollar!"

It was going to be another long August day on the Olson farm. Everyone was busy with harvesting and Nadia loved being right in the thick of things. Ray always said that he didn't need to bother with hired hands; he had Kevin and Nadia.

The Olsons lived on a farm in northern Minnesota, four miles from the Canadian border. They grew small grains: oats, wheat, and flax. They also had a small herd of beef cattle. This year the hay crop was bountiful so the cattle would be well-fed all winter. If the weather continued to be warm and dry they should complete the thrashing in a few days, except for the flax. Nadia was dreaming of the day she wouldn't be awakened by Kevin's "Sun's up, let's go." On this day, Mary was busy making a hearty breakfast for her crew—pancakes, eggs and bacon. There was no need to worry about cholesterol or calories on the farm—they would be taken care of throughout the day. Nadia's food intake was that of a man's but she worked hard, so why did she have a weight problem?

Nadia was seventeen soon to be eighteen and a senior in high school. She was tall with thick, beautiful brown hair that hung to her waist, great skin, and perfect teeth. One problem: she could not get rid of the extra twenty pounds she carried. Deniably, she wasn't fat; "plump" would be the word to describe her. She worked like a dog, so no one could understand why she wasn't razor thin. Nadia loved the outdoors—enjoyed anything that involved farming, hunting and fishing. She was Dad's "boy."

Mary and Ray had four children: Jackie, Ginny, Kevin and Nadia. Jackie and Ginny were Mom's girls. They enjoyed doing anything and everything that women were traditionally supposed to do: cooking, baking, cleaning, sewing and shopping. Both of them were intelligent, thin and blonde with blue eyes and fair skin. They ate everything they cooked and never gained a pound! Boys in the community hung around the farm all of the time for the food but if they were really trying to impress the girls, they would throw a few bales. They would always take time to visit with Kevin and the "farm girl" as they had so aptly named Nadia. Jackie especially played along, although she had no interest in having a boyfriend. She was in her final year at Bemidji State College and had big plans after graduation. Jackie had applied to the Peace Corps with the Philippines as her first choice. Jackie knew that in order to be accepted by the Peace Corps, she had to have a perfect background—nothing on her driving record, no arrests for drugs or alcohol and an above average grade point in college. She met all of the requirements so her acceptance was almost guaranteed. Also included in her plans was a desire to travel around Southeast Asia. Ray and Mary weren't happy with Jackie's plans, but they knew her personality and realized they would have to accept them.

Ginny was Miss Personality. She wanted to be surrounded by family and friends all of the time. The more friends she could have at the farm, the better. Boys or girls, it didn't matter. Her love of baking only enhanced her popularity. Every boy in school loved to drive out because they knew that homemade cookies, pies, bars or cake would always be offered to them. Her looks were also a drawing card: blonde hair, blue eyes, five feet six inches, nice bosom, tiny waist, 120 pounds—good to look at. She had only one problem: her older sister. Jackie was a straight A student. Ginny was smart, but not as smart as Jackie.

All during high school the teachers were constantly comparing them. "Why aren't you trying?" Why don't you take school more seriously like Jackie did?" It seemed the more the teachers harassed her, the less she studied. She had looked forward to graduation day because in college no one would even know that Jackie existed; she could be her own person. Ginny ended up graduating seventh in her class of 99—not bad, considering that she was Ray and Mary's social butterfly.

Kevin—Nadia's hero—was tall, blonde and good-looking, a hard worker, a Christian and a fantastic baseball player. For three fourths of the year he worked his heart out on the farm. In the spring though, once baseball started, Ray cut him slack. "Baseball practice is just as important as farming," he said. Ray would be out in the fields from sunup to sundown. The only time he would take off was when the Chiefs played baseball at home. Kevin was the catcher and a good one. Every year on the first day of practice the coach would marvel at what excellent shape Kevin was in. Ray and Mary were ardent fans, but it was Nadia who saw and remembered every hit, run and error. Kevin was not only her big brother, he was her hero. The feeling was mutual. He loved his little sister. He protected Nadia and watched over her like no other. On evenings after practice and games, the other boys on the team wanted him to "go out on the town." Only after he had made sure Nadia was occupied and happy with her friends or at home would he accept. Kevin had no qualms about anyone knowing that he loved to go to church, taught Sunday School, and helped with Vacation Bible School. His friends never made fun of him; instead, they would find ways they could also help. Nadia was watchful of everything he did. He was her role model.

Nadia smiled when she thought about one family that benefited from Kevin's compassion. It was a family in town that had seven children. The father worked two jobs to keep the family going. The mother couldn't work outside the home because she had Parkinson's disease. The oldest boy, Roger, was the same age as Kevin. When he was thirteen, he was helping his dad change the oil on the car and the jack disengaged, which caused the fender to fall on his hand and cut off three fingers. The doctors were not able to reattach them. Roger shared Kevin's passion for baseball but, because of his disability, he couldn't play. Kevin convinced the coach that Roger would make a great bat boy, and in later years he became the assistant coach. He received no pay but that wasn't necessary. Wearing a jersey with "Coach" stitched on it was payment enough. For four years, Kevin picked him up and brought him home every day there was practice or a game. On graduation day, Roger was the class speaker. Several times in his speech he used Kevin as an example. "Kevin taught me what it means to be a friend, what it means to be a good person, and, most importantly, how keeping God in our daily lives can make life so much easier." His touching speech brought tears to all who were in attendance. Nadia sat with tears flowing and a smile that covered her face. Silently she said, "That's my brother. I want to be exactly like him: loving, caring and giving." She was pensive every time the thought of him leaving for college entered her mind.

Knowing some things about the Olson family, one can understand how difficult it is when each child leaves the nest. This year Nadia would be home alone with her parents. She knew how important it was to finish the harvesting. So now, on Saturday everyone was working hard. Ray was swathing oats; Kevin was combining the last of the wheat; and Nadia was driving the truck to and from the field, emptying the seed into the steel bin. It was hot: 89 degrees at eleven o'clock in the morning. It was supposed to reach 93 degrees by two o'clock. There was no rain in the forecast for the next five days. If this held, it meant they could finish the harvesting except for the flax, which wouldn't be ready for another three weeks. Ray and Kevin had everything planned out. Kevin would come home from college to help finish the harvest. That way Ray could combine, Nadia could haul it directly to the elevator in town, and Kevin would bale the flax straw.

Part 1

It was a little more than a week before school started for everyone. Mary, Ginny and Jackie stayed busy preparing huge lunches, which they would take to the field so work wouldn't have to stop for long. On the menu for this day were chicken breasts on homemade bread, jello salad with sliced bananas, potato salad, cake, coffee and a gallon of ice cold water. During the heat of the day, it was the water the guys most welcomed.

On Tuesday morning, Nadia went to school to check the class list in the principal's office. She was taking a full load. Besides the regular classes, she had signed up for two college courses. She had planned her college years and in order to finish "on time" she needed to take some general courses in high school. Nadia's goal was to have her doctorate in psychology as soon as possible. Her schedule was perfect; it even allowed her to participate in band. The school advisor had thought that maybe she'd have to quit band in order to fit everything in, which wouldn't have been the end of the world, except this was the year the band took its trip to New York and Washington, D.C.

After meeting all her friends, Nadia had to run; the truck would be full and would need to be emptied. A good harvest meant that life would be much easier in the winter, especially for her Dad who wouldn't have to cut pulp. Her mother hated when he'd go to the woods by himself to cut huge spruce trees. The dangers of the chain saw slipping, trees falling the wrong way, her Dad tripping while walking to and from the warming shack with no way to call for help—they created constant worry. Many, many prayers were sent upward on the days that Ray cut pulp alone.

On Sunday, immediately after church, the Olsons left to take Jackie to Bemidji and then on to Moorhead to drop off Ginny. College classes started for both of them the following week. Kevin wouldn't have to leave for college until Wednesday. To make the trip more fun, they packed a picnic lunch, which they enjoyed on the beach at Lake Bemidji. The whole family shed tears as they waved goodbye to Jackie. She would graduate in December but wouldn't actually get her diploma until May. Jackie was hoping by that time she would be heading for the Philippines. Sentimental Ginny was more tentative about saying goodbye. She made three trips back to the car, crying uncontrollably. Her chances of getting back home before Christmas break were slim, since none of her classmates had joined her in Moorhead, and she would have no ride. Nadia told her not to worry. She would write twice a week, and Ray told her to call every Friday night. It was 2:00 in the morning before Nadia, Kevin, Ray and Mary reached home.

Monday was the last day of combining, and they finished at 3 o'clock. Needless to say, everyone was so tired they were in bed by 8:30 that night.

Mary had to be in school for in-service on Tuesday morning. This was her 20th year of teaching fifth grade at the public school. She enjoyed teaching and the students loved her. She made learning fun, was fair, and believed that homework wasn't necessary if a student worked during class hours. The request list from parents to have their children in her classroom was always long. The principal had a tough job every fall trying to pare down the list without making anyone angry.

Ray and Kevin plowed the fields while Nadia made lunch. She detested cooking of any kind, so everyone was glad that Mary would be home to prepare supper.

On Wednesday, Nadia and Ray dropped Kevin off at his apartment near the college in Thief River Falls, after having dinner at McDonalds. This was the first time that Nadia had seen her Dad cry. She knew what he was thinking: His son was no longer a child; he was an adult and on his own. Nadia drove home and Ray spoke very little. When they arrived home, the first thing Nadia noticed was how quiet the Olson home was—too quiet. She went upstairs to her room and cried herself to sleep. Her big brother, caretaker, friend and ally had left. How would or could she ever enjoy her senior year? The next few days passed quickly, however, and the home front gradually returned to normal. Phone calls from all of the kids erased the pain of losing Kevin. Life went on!

On the following Monday morning Mary and Nadia left for school. Ray was going to do some cultivating. Buford, the family dog, became his constant companion, even riding for hours on the tractor platform that Ray had made for him to lie on. Kevin got a good laugh when he heard that he had been replaced by the dog!

The first day of school went fine. Nadia had cheerleading tryouts immediately after school. Mary worked in her classroom so they could ride home together after the tryouts. Nadia didn't really want to try out. She felt that her chances of making the squad were slim because of her weight problem. But she executed all of the jumps, hand stands and line dances perfectly, and her voice was loud and clear—so she felt good about her tryout. The judges would post the list of cheerleaders the next morning.

Sleep didn't come easily that night. Nadia wanted to make the squad for two reasons: it would fill the time without Kevin, and

Mary and Ray would have a good reason to go to the football, hockey and baseball games.

It turned out that Nadia not only made the squad, she was named captain. At that exact moment she made a deal with herself: She would lose those twenty pounds. She went to Mary's room to tell her the good news and her decision.

"Mom, I made the squad and I want to lose weight. Will you help me?"

Mary readily replied, "Of course I will." She didn't have any doubt that Nadia would lose the weight because when Nadia made up her mind to do something, it happened. With all of the fresh vegetables from the garden, healthy low-calorie meals would be easy to prepare.

The Olson farm was located four miles from town. Nadia planned to practice after school and then run home. It would be great exercise and no one would have to drive her home from practice.

The cheerleaders practiced long and hard for the first football game on Friday night. They were pumped up. They all believed that the football team would be good so it would be easy to cheer and get the crowd into the game. Their uniforms, pompoms, and flags were distributed; their jumps, dances, and cheers were perfected. They were ready!

Mary and Ray were proud supporters of their children in all of their endeavors. They realized that this would be the last year to follow one of their children in high school sports.

Ray worked until sundown finishing up the fields on Friday. He cut the flax and knew it would be ready for harvesting on Saturday. Kevin wouldn't be home but Ray, Nadia, and Mary would be fine. As usual, the weather would determine if he would finish in one day.

The Chiefs defeated the Bears, 17-3. The game was exciting and nail-biting until the last quarter when the Chiefs scored two touchdowns in the final minutes. Their next game would be

Homecoming. Nadia was in the Top Ten nominated for queen. The festivities would begin with the coronation on Monday evening so, along with the business on the farm, Mary was engaged in sewing a dress for Nadia. The dress turned out to be exquisite! Mary and Nadia had seen it in a magazine but the cost was out of their price line, so they purchased the material, cut out the picture, and Mary used her expertise to replicate it perfectly. Nadia put it on for a final fitting. Ray and Mary sat in the living room awaiting "the show." Tears rolled. Nadia was beautiful in the spaghetti-strapped, knee length red dress, and Ray and Mary were once again reminded that this was the last year of high school grandeur.

Saturday was a busy day. Kevin was able to get a ride home with friends and surprised his parents and Nadia with a visit. He arrived at the farm just as Ray was heading out on the combine. His presence meant that Nadia didn't have to help Ray. It was a great day: wonderful weather, no mechanical problems, and a completed harvest. The family didn't sit down for supper until 9:00. The mood around the table was exciting. It had been a fabulous year for the farmers, a year to catch up on the bills and stash a little away for a rainy day.

Mary was tired all of the time. Everyone attributed it to her busy schedule, but in her heart she felt it was something more serious. She kept up the hectic pace of being a mother, wife, seamstress, canner, cook, baker and teacher. Each day she looked more tired and rundown. Ray was worried about her.

On Monday evening Ray and Mary went to the coronation. The gym was packed to the ceiling. The girls were beautiful and the candidates for king were handsome in their best suits. All of the candidates were introduced, and then it was time for the big event. The master of ceremony announced the third and second attendants and then only two lovely ladies remained on stage: Nadia and her best friend, Ali. When Ali was announced as the first attendant, Nadia knew that she would be crowned

Homecoming Queen in 1970. She and the king made their walk down the aisle. Nadia found Ray and Mary and gave them each a huge hug and then returned to her friends.

Suddenly there was a tremendous commotion in the crowd. Everyone seemed to be shouting at once. "Dr. Ken, Dr. Ken, hurry!"

The doctor rushed over to where Mary was slumped over Ray who yelled, "Call the ambulance!"

Nadia ran over to her mother. "Mom, Mom, please talk to me. Please, Mom!"

Dr. Ken was by her mother's side when the ambulance arrived. They took Mary to the hospital in a neighboring town. Ray and Nadia followed. By the time they got to the hospital, Mary was in the ER. The waiting room at the hospital was soon filled with concerned people—parents and students, the entire football team, the cheerleading squad, Pastor Jim, and the principal. After what seemed like a lifetime, Dr. Ken came out and delivered some very good news.

"Mary is suffering from total exhaustion. She is resting comfortably, and we'll be keeping her here to do some tests. Ray and Nadia, she wants to see both of you."

Prayers of thanks were said around the room. Nadia turned to the crowd and thanked everyone for their love and concern. She promised to keep them up to date. Feeling total relief and blessedness, Nadia and Ray refused to leave Mary that night. The nurse brought in two reclining chairs and blankets where they both got some intermittent sleep.

Jackie, Ginny, and Kevin arrived later that night. Nadia's date for homecoming had his father, who was the police chief, locate each of them, and then he drove to Bemidji, Grand Forks (Ginny's friend drove her there), and Thief River Falls to pick them up. No one could put into words the relief and comfort Ray and Nadia felt when the rest of the family entered the room.

Everyone found places to sleep in the waiting room. After two more days of tests and rest, Mary was sent home with strict orders from Dr. Ken: no school and no work at home for the rest of the week.

Mary was dismayed at the doctor's orders. The rest of the corn and tomatoes had to be canned, and her students would miss her. In the twenty years of teaching, she had accumulated over 300 sick days, so staying home wasn't a problem, but she hated to do that.

There was no need for her to worry! The following day, three neighbor ladies showed up at the door. They picked, cleaned and canned all the corn and tomatoes. They even took the time to can twenty-four jars of salsa. Their generosity was one of the joys of living in a small town! Mary received dozens of cards, many of them homemade, from her students this year and from previous years.

The older kids went back to college on Wednesday and Nadia went back to school, cheerleading practice and running. Ray put the finishing touchups around the farm.

On Friday night Nadia felt secure enough to go to the Homecoming dance with her long-time friend, Andy. Neither of them expected their relationship to go beyond friendship. She liked Andy; he reminded her of Kevin. At 10:00 he asked Nadia if she'd like to check on her mother. They slipped out of the dance and zipped home. Nadia ran into the house to find her parents sitting in the living room watching the baseball game. That was the wrong thing for her to see! She was a Twins fan from the word go. She had never had the opportunity to go to a game because the tickets were too high and the timing was wrong for someone who was busy with work on a farm. Andy knocked on the door thinking that something was wrong. Mary saw him and told Nadia she had to leave. The debate was on: Should they finish watching the game or go back to the dance?

The Twins were ahead in the eighth inning by a large margin, so the dance won out. They arrived back at the gym just as the royalty dance was to begin.

The rest of the fall was business as usual. Mary went back to school; Ray kept busy around the farm; and Nadia's days were filled with studying, cheerleading and running. As a senior, she knew that she would be taking either the SAT or the ACT in a few weeks. At this point, she didn't know which she should take, since she didn't know for sure where she would be going to college.

Nadia had lost ten pounds. Mary packed their lunches every day, filling the lunch boxes with fresh cucumbers, tomatoes, homemade bread and slices of chicken. Nadia kept running and started working out in the weight room. Her goal was to weigh 130 pounds on November first. At five feet, seven inches she felt this was the perfect weight. As the pounds came off, Nadia's self esteem and confidence grew; she was even speaking out more in class. She thought that maybe she could get into the University of Minnesota, so she had Mary help her with the application. Now all she had to do was wait and watch for the letter to arrive. Nadia had an ulterior motive for wanting to go to Minneapolis: She would be close to where the Twins played. She thought constantly about the University deal for college students: They could attend a game for $1.00 if they presented their university identification card. Each time she thought about that, her excitement grew.

Autumn was a beautiful time of year in northern Minnesota. An abundance of yellow, orange and red leaves replaced the green ones. Ray planned a trip to the Superior National Forest during the long MEA weekend in October when Mary was free. Even though he felt it was impossible for Ginny, Jackie, and Kevin to join them, he called and told them about the plan anyway. He explained that the trip would take place the same weekend as the Harvest Festival at church.

Ray had a deep and lasting desire for his family to be together as often as possible; he was always working toward that goal, it seemed. He knew that Jackie would be gone next year to the Peace Corps, and the rest would be in college. This possibly would be the last time a trip of this kind could happen. To the surprise of everyone, all three of the absent children called and said they'd be able to go on the trip. Ray and Mary were excited and loved making plans, including hotel reservations. They would stay in Duluth on Friday night and in a motel on the North Shore on Saturday night. Nadia was ecstatic—everyone together!

The entire family enjoyed the football game which was played on Thursday night instead of the usual Friday because of the fall break. At this point in the season the Chiefs were 50-50: not as good as was expected. They lost to their rival, the Angels. It was a close game, but they couldn't muster enough offense at the end. Nadia and her weight loss was a topic of conversation during the game. Everyone noticed and approved.

On Friday morning the Olsons loaded the car and drove off at 8:00. It was crowded: six adults and luggage filled the family car. But no one seemed to mind; laughter and stories abounded and drew them close together as a family. The Olsons felt that there was nothing in this world more important than an entire family being together. During the trip, the children were struck by Ray's desire to protect Mary. He wanted her to relax and enjoy the weekend. Any task that had to be done was done by him or one of the kids. Mary usually used the MEA long weekend to clean the house from top to bottom. This included washing all the windows inside and out, cleaning the carpets, washing the curtains, waxing the hardwood floors, scrubbing the walls—it all had to be done. While she was wondering how it would get done, Ray was making plans to hire people to come in and complete the cleaning list she had compiled. When the children were told of his plan, it sank in how truly good the harvest had been. Paying someone to clean house—never been done before!

Their vacation was exciting. The four kids walked miles along the North Shore. When they sat down to rest before heading back, a penetrating scream came out of Kevin's mouth. A garden snake had crawled up his pant leg. He jumped up trying to get the snake to fall out; instead it wrapped itself around his leg. Kevin tore off his pants and danced around. When the episode was over, the three girls laughed so hard tears ran down their faces. It took Kevin a good half hour to calm down. To this day, he sees no humor in this story.

On Saturday evening they went to dinner at a beautiful restaurant that was nestled in the pines next to the lake. The Olsons didn't go out to eat very often so this was a real treat. Ray ordered a T-bone steak; Mary decided on the salmon; Ginny, Jackie and Nadia ordered the grilled chicken salad and French onion soup. Kevin debated a long time and finally decided that the filet mignon sounded the best. When the waitress set Ray's big beautiful T-bone down and then proceeded to give Kevin a silver dollar size filet, the look on his face was priceless. Kevin could have eaten the entire filet in two bites, but he took his time and enjoyed the taste, as long as it lasted. After the snickers subsided, the family enjoyed their meal.

Rest and relaxation were an important part of the three days which closed with a shopping spree in Duluth. Ray and Kevin went to Cabela's and the women to the mall. Mary found material to start another quilt and the three girls each bought a new outfit and shoes. They arrived home in time to get ready for the Harvest Festival, which they all enjoyed immensely. A group, God's Messengers, provided the music and message.

Ray left home at 4:00 a.m. on Monday to take the college kids back. He dropped Kevin off first, then on to Bemidji for Jackie, and from there to Moorhead where he and Ginny enjoyed breakfast at McDonalds. He took a large coffee to go; it would be a long ride home.

The home front was deserted when Ray got there. Mary and Nadia had left for school. He made himself some coffee and went outside.

The Chiefs played their game of the season, handicapped by injuries to two of their players. They were defeated and the season was over. School was unusually quiet. The hockey and basketball season wouldn't begin for three weeks, but there was no downtime for the cheerleaders. Nadia went to practice and continued to run and work out. Her weight went down; she weighed 134 on the 15th of October with only four pounds to go. Everyone told her when she began this project that anyone could lose weight but keeping it off was the bigger challenge. It would be especially difficult when she started college; the "freshman fifteen" was almost a guarantee. But Nadia had made up her mind: Once these extra pounds were gone, they would never find their way back to her body. She reasoned that there were sidewalks, paths and roads to run on in Minneapolis, so she would reach her goal. Period!

Nadia spent a lot of with her two friends, Ali and Andy. They didn't party or drink and they went to the same church. Their values in life were the same. Right now they were making plans to attend the Christian Rally for Teens in Minneapolis on the Friday and Saturday after Thanksgiving. The church made it clear that anyone who would like to attend would have his transportation and hotel costs taken care of. Thousands of teens were expected to attend. The three of them plus seven more juniors and seniors had signed up. Ray and Mary offered to drive as did Andy's parents.

Jackie received her acceptance from the Peace Corps and would be leaving the first of January. She made a list of all the things she'd need for the two years. Mary felt that the weekend in Minneapolis would be a good opportunity for her to shop and shorten the list. The climate in the Philippines was 100 percent different than that of Northern Minnesota, with high heat and humidity—so she would need light clothing. Also, the Filipinos were generally small people while Jackie was tall with quite a large bosom, so she needed to buy bras before she left the States.

The older Nadia grew, the more she realized how efficient Mary was. She was always two steps ahead of anyone else and could get more done in a short period of time than anyone Nadia knew. Every item on Jackie's list had been taken care of before they left Minneapolis.

The Major League Playoffs were winding down. The Twins had been beaten in the second round by the Yankees. The games were on TV but the interest just wasn't there. Ray and Mary kept saying that someday the Twins would win the World Series. It just wasn't going to be this year.

November 4th was D-Day. Nadia stepped on the scale—130 pounds! She was proud that she had reached this goal for herself. With her new self-confidence, she was surpassing her expectations at school—straight As on her report cards with notations on the side from many teachers. One in particular was very compelling: "Hard worker, dedicated, confident, devoted—she will be successful."

Ali and Nadia spent hours together. Ali received her acceptance to the University of Minnesota Duluth. Nadia was still waiting for her letter. Ray allowed the two of them to take the family car to Grand Forks. Nadia definitely needed new clothes; her old ones were baggy and hung on her slim body. Ray gave Nadia $200 to spend. She was stunned: never had she had so much money in her possession! The entire day was fun. They felt like adults—a car, money, time, choices, all on their own. The first stop was at Kevin's college in Thief River. A genuine look of pride came over his face when he walked out of class and saw them standing there. With him were two young men who wanted to be introduced.

Kevin wouldn't hear of it. "No way, this is my baby sister and her friend. Both of them are great girls. You're not going to have a chance to tarnish them in any way."

The reactions to Kevin's warning were pretty much expected: giggles from Ali and Nadia; disgusted looks from the two guys; and laughter from Kevin himself.

Nadia delivered the letter to Kevin from their parents. Two $50 bills fell to the floor. The note read, "Life on the farm was good this year. Take this money and buy something special. We love you." With that, Nadia and Ali left him and drove on to Grand Forks.

Shopping was fun. Nadia bought two pairs of jeans, a pair of khakis, three lovely tops, a burgundy sweatshirt with a University of Minnesota logo (she was probably counting her chickens before they had hatched), socks, underwear, hair scrunchies, make-up and a treat for her parents. The $200 from her Dad didn't quite cover all of it, so she used the money she had saved from helping her uncle spray the crops last summer. She also used some of the money she was paid for helping paint the police station. "Money in the bank," she had kept reminding herself when the sweat ran down her back. On their way out of town, they stopped at Scheels where both Nadia and Ali bought a swimsuit with matching bag and towel. Neither one of them had ever owned a two-piece bathing suit before, and the ones they bought now were colorful, but definitely conservative by teenage standards. They filled their car with gas, picked up a Diet Coke and a bag of beef jerky and headed home.

Ray and Mary were relieved when they spotted the car coming down the driveway at 10:00 that night. They couldn't figure out how two young girls could spend so much time shopping.

The first snow fell a few days before Thanksgiving. It was a beautiful sight. Even though winters are long, Northern Minnesotans love the new white stuff covering everything—fallen leaves, brown grass, and dead flowers. The blanket of white provided so much beauty.

Winter on a farm is peaceful. Ray uses this time to fix the machinery and feed the beef cattle a couple of bales of hay every other day. This winter he was going to work on the basement, one of the many projects he wanted to complete. It was a large area but with four children, the money was never available to fix it. Mary had her laundry room, sewing room and fruit cellar down there. He planned to put up walls to divide these rooms, build a suspended ceiling, and carpet the entire area. Nadia couldn't help but recognize the irony. When everyone was home the extra room was needed. Now all four children would soon be gone and they won't need the extra room, but they can now afford to remodel.

Mary was sewing a log cabin quilt for each of the kids for Christmas. To give her enough time to complete the task, Nadia took over the chores of cooking supper and doing the dishes. She actually enjoyed this. Normally, Jackie and Ginny were the "cookers and bakers" when they were home, but now that they weren't home, Nadia had to learn the secrets of preparing tasty and healthy meals. Some of hers had been pretty scary of late, such as the meat loaf. Mary's always fell out of the pan in a perfect loaf; Nadia's came out in big globs of meat surrounded by too much juice because she had forgotten to add the soda crackers. She also burned potatoes in the pot; her spaghetti noodles stuck together in a ball; and her chili was so spicy even Buford wouldn't eat it. She improved a lot over the winter.

Ray had requested that Mary prepare game hens for Thanksgiving dinner. A huge smile covered his face when they sat down to eat and his wish had come true. Life was good!

Andy, Ali and Nadia rode with Ray and Mary to the Youth Convention. The caravan from Northern Minnesota didn't arrive at the hotel in Minneapolis until 12:30 a.m. They hoped that sleep would come quickly, since the convention began at the early hour of eight o'clock. They split up the girls and boys into two rooms. One can only imagine five teenage girls trying to get ready in one bathroom. Hair dryers and straighteners, curling irons, make-up, hair spray, perfume, tooth brushes, combs, hairbrushes—so much stuff it would be impossible to keep track of what belonged to whom. At 7:55 the next morning, they all got off the elevator to be greeted by unbelievable music. The welcoming committee consisted of a band with three drummers, two electric guitars, three electric organs, and four young men singing, "Our God is an Awesome God" over and over again. A huge sign hung behind the band. It said:

"If Jesus won't say it, I won't say it.

If Jesus won't do it, I won't do it.

If Jesus won't go there, I won't go there."

What a statement! Nadia immediately asked herself if she could live up to that commitment. The five thousand young people in attendance were awake, vibrant and boisterous. It was a magical moment. No, it was a magical forty-eight hours. Sleep was non-existent, but no one cared. Sleep could come when everyone said good-bye and went on his or her own way. Nadia felt peace, serenity, and contentment when she left. How would she ever be able to spread the message of God's love to everyone she met? She didn't have the answer; she only knew that she would give it her all.

The trip home provided time to reflect and reminisce, to plan for the future, and grab a few minutes of sleep. The Olsons dropped off Ali and Andy and pulled into their driveway at 11:00. The house was a welcome sight. They each carried in a suitcase and decided that the rest of the stuff in the car could be unloaded in the morning.

The phone was ringing as Ray was unlocking the door. Nadia was in first so she grabbed it. It was Andy.

"Nadia, there's been a horrible accident. The Amisons were hit head on by a drunk driver. Everyone was killed."

There was complete, total, and eerie silence. Nadia hung up the phone. In a barely audible voice she told her parents what had happened.

Ray spoke first, "We have to go. Where exactly, I don't know, but we have to go someplace."

Back in the car they headed for Andy's house. There must have been three dozen cars parked everywhere. News as horrible as this travels quickly in a small town. Before they exited the vehicle, they prayed together with tears flowing like waterfalls.

The Amisons were turning into the a restaurant. They were waiting for a vehicle to pass when it struck them head on. The highway patrolman knew this because one of the passengers lived long enough to tell them the story. They knew from the impact that the driver of the pick-up was going between eighty and ninety miles an hour. He never hit the brakes.

The love, joy and contentment Nadia had felt a few hours earlier were replaced with hatred, sadness and resentment. Why would God ever allow something like this to happen, especially now, just as they were coming home from an uplifting gathering of God's teenagers? Nadia knew better than to ask why, she just couldn't think of anything else to ponder. Their small town, their school, their community—would they ever heal? Three families' lives had been changed forever.

As the days passed, they learned more about the man who caused the crash. He was twenty-three and had just come off the road after being gone for ninety days. His wife had left him a note on the table saying she wanted a divorce. She had taken both of their little boys, ages seven and four, back to Canada. The note ended with the command: "Do not under any circumstances try to call them or come to see them." He had left the house with a bottle of whiskey, a bottle of rum and ten bottles of beer. He had driven sixty-two miles while drinking. Two empty bottles were found under the passenger seat. Seven empty beer cans were also lying on the floor. Two were unopened and one was sitting upright between his legs. Three months after the accident they still hadn't located his family in Canada.

This was supposed to be a festive month. The first day of December marked the traditional beginning of practicing for the church Christmas pageant. "Jesus is the Reason for the Season" was the play for this year. Sunday School children started preparing for their programs; the band and choir at school put on concerts; the hockey team had just completed their jamboree—but no one really felt like doing anything. Instead, the focus was on making preparations for funerals, which were held in the school gymnasium all at the same time. Mr. Amison had been the school principal and Mrs. Amison an English teacher in the high school. Two of the students who lost their lives were juniors and three were seniors. All of them were church members. This was the first time Nadia saw Pastor Jim cry.

Jackie, Ginny and Kevin came home to attend the funerals on Friday. Pastor Jim asked two pastors from neighboring churches to help him. The gym was filled to capacity; mourners filled the school cafeteria and the halls. The high school band played "How Great Thou Art" over and over while the ushers seated everyone. The service was beautifully done. Pastor Jim gave an inspiring sermon and the school choir sang "Amazing Grace" better than Nadia had ever heard it sung before. People kept saying the funeral would bring closure. Closure to what? Did this mean that as soon as the funerals were over they'd forget about their friends? Nadia's response was "Stupid statement, stupid people." The sadness in the lives of the town people continued throughout the Christmas season.

On December 16th, Nadia received her acceptance letter from the University of Minnesota. She was incredibly happy but there was an underlying feeling of "why me?" The five students who died were good people. They would never have the opportunity to attend college. Mary constantly reminded Nadia that the students who died were much happier now than ever before. Whenever something good happened in Nadia's life, it seemed that she asked the same question: "Why me?"

Depression was rampant at school. The best psychologists in the country offered their services to the students. Christmas activities came and went. The concerts, pageants and programs were all held, but with little enthusiasm. Nadia's weight dropped to 120 pounds.

On Christmas Eve the Olsons had their usual lutefisk, bar-b-que ribs, mashed potatoes, lefse, baked squash and glorified rice. The family tried to make the evening fun and festive. They exchanged gifts and went to midnight services at the church where they sang the old familiar Christmas carols. This year though, it was hard to sing the carols enthusiastically—even to get excited about the gifts.

Santa Claus came when everyone was sleeping, true to tradition. He was especially imaginative this year, having sewn four gorgeous quilts with perfect colors for each of the children. He also brought the family three Arctic Cat snowmobiles: two Panthers and a Jag. The Panther could fit two people. Everyone immediately recognized a problem—who would stay at home when they had a family snocatting expedition? The grin on Ray's face was so large you could have placed a banana crosswise in it.

"Put your jackets on and follow me."

Everyone trudged through the snow and entered the work shed. There, sitting in the middle of the room was the most beautiful black and green sled you could ever imagine. It was enclosed with windows on the sides and front. Engraved on the dash was one word: "Mary." Everyone admired it, sat in it, and questioned Ray as to how he had managed to make something like this without anyone knowing. Mary couldn't speak for several seconds. All the while, Ray sat with that goofy grin on his face. The family strolled back to the house and enjoyed a breakfast fit for a king, prepared by Jackie and Ginny. Kevin was the first to suggest that they clean up the kitchen, pack a couple of thermoses of coffee and leftover Christmas cookies, and take a long ride in the woods.

The trails were groomed and, with three inches of fresh snowfall, snocatting was perfect. They spent five hours in the woods, witnessing beauty at its finest. Deer—twenty-two of them—also enjoyed the beautiful day. Four rabbits, adorned in their winter white coats, delighted the snocatters with their game of hide and seek. Nadia thought that if anyone on this earth had been with them and still questioned God's hand in creating the world, it would be impossible for her to understand. It was beauty beyond anyone's imagination.

On Christmas Day evening, the Olsons delivered meals and gifts to each family that had been touched by the accident. They also spent hours at the Community Center with people less fortunate than they, especially people without families to enjoy the holiday season. Two older gentlemen who had lost their wives refused to go anywhere for Christmas except the Center. There were children present because of problems caused by divorce. In one case, a father had lost his job a month before Christmas. The community rallied together and collected "Santa" gifts. The excitement and happiness around the room made the evening a real success.

The next few days were spent working in the basement and plowing roads—including their own and the driveways of their neighbors. Snow fell for two days, so about seven inches of the white fluff accumulated. The snocats never had a chance to cool off. Nadia's friends hung around in droves. Andy forgot where home was. He loved spending time with Kevin and Ray, mostly ice fishing for walleye. Most of the time they brought home their limits. A large fish fry was held the evening before everyone headed back to college. Time went by too quickly.

Kevin had spent a fair amount of time talking about Katie while he was home. Of the three children heading back to college, he was the most excited to get going. Once again, Ray drove each of them to their destinations. Mary chose to stay home; she wanted to get the house back in order before going back to school. Nadia rode with Ray; she couldn't imagine him driving home alone. Moorhead was their first stop. Poor Ginny started crying when they left home and never stopped until they dropped her off at the dorm. They took the freeway to Bemidji where Kevin and Ray made several trips to load up all of Jackie's belongings. Her college days were over, and she was about to begin the next phase of her life.

The closer they got to Thief River, the more talkative Kevin became. Eventually, he made the statement everyone was sure he had wanted to make during the entire vacation.

"There's going to be someone at my apartment that I want all of you to meet." He was so serious.

When they pulled up to the apartment building they immediately saw, standing in the doorway, the young lady who was the light of Kevin's life. The moment Kevin saw her, a smile crossed his face. Ray had barely stopped the car when Kevin was out the door. They were shocked that he showed such affection right in front of them. This girl must be special, because he usually reserved those hugs for his mother and sisters. Nadia thought, "Move over, Mom and Sisters—there's another woman in Kevin's life!"

"Dad, Jackie, and Nadia, I want you to meet Katie. Katie, this is my family minus a sister and my Mom."

The reception they received from Katie was warm and friendly. It took only a few minutes of speaking to her for them to realize that she would probably be a part of Kevin's life and therefore a part of the family.

Life at the Olson home was anything but boring. One change or another was always in the making. Jackie was making plans to leave for the Philippines on the 7th of January. She would fly from Minneapolis to Hawaii, spend three weeks there in training, and then proceed to Manila where her host family and two colleagues from the Peace Corps would meet her. She would have two weeks to get acquainted with her family and surroundings. After that, her two-year commitment would begin.

Mary and Nadia went back to school on Tuesday. With the wind chill, the temperature outside was 39 degrees below zero. Normally, students left the school during their lunch hour; today everyone hung out inside the school. No one had the zeal to go outside to start their cars, warm them up, and drive to the local gas station to get a treat. It definitely was much easier to consume their lunch at school or skip lunch all together and hang out in the library or gym.

The Chiefs were scheduled to play their biggest rival in hockey. Even though the weather was horrific, the arena was packed. Northern Minnesotans were a hardy bunch, however, so they wouldn't think of staying home for the biggest game of the year. Nadia and Mary rushed home from school to get ready for the game. Ginny had made lasagna (her specialty) when she was home. Dinner was eaten quickly, so they could all get to the arena in time.

The scene at the arena was a jumbled mess. Twelve hundred people were trying to get through the door at once. The moment the puck was dropped the evening was a disaster in the making. The Rams scored in the first minute, and it only got worse. The final score was 12-2. It was hard to cheer for the home team when the score was so lopsided. The Chiefs had graduated seven seniors and knew this was going to be a rebuilding year and a long season for the hockey fans but they had hoped to avoid slaughter. The Olsons wanted to leave via the back door but decided that only "losers" did that. Last year when the Chiefs beat the Rams in both games, they proudly stuck around and quietly "rubbed it in their faces." Tonight they exited as quickly as possible.

Winter droned on. Snow, freezing temperatures and wind prevented the Olson family from doing much snocatting. Usually the weather moderated in March, and they were counting on that being the case this year so they'd get to resume their winter activities. For now it was start the car, warm it up, get in to where you were going, and stay there.

After finishing touches were made for Jackie's new adventure, the family left for Minneapolis early on Saturday morning. Emotions were running high. Jackie was excited and ready to take on anything. She had been anticipating this moment for three years. Mary was reluctant to have her oldest daughter half way around the world for two years. She kept repeating to herself, "We'll put everything in God's hands." Nadia was reminded once again of Mary's unshakable faith.

Once they were in the airport Jackie handed Nadia her winter coat. "I won't be needing this for a couple of years. It's hard to imagine leaving Minneapolis where it's 26 degrees below zero and landing in Honolulu where it is 80 degrees."

Jackie's plane departed right on time. The rest of the family stood quietly and watched until it was only a speck in the sky. Jackie promised she'd call when she landed in Hawaii.

The trip home was frightening. Each time a car approached everyone would tense up. The memories of the crash and death of their friends were still fresh in their minds. They were filled with relief when they drove the car into the garage. It wasn't long after they arrived home that Jackie called from Hawaii. She said that her trip had been uneventful and she was fine.

Winter plugged along and so did the Olsons. Most of the month of January was spent indoors. Once home and in the nice, warm house, no one wanted to leave. Ginny and Kevin weren't coming home until spring break at the end of March. "Boring" was the word that described life, according to Nadia.

Nadia put on two pounds. For all the years her weight had been excessive, it wasn't a problem now; 120 pounds on a 5'7" frame was low. Her friends were convinced that she was anorexic. She wasn't. She ate three meals a day. Maybe she remained thin because she stayed active. She and Ray completed the remodeling of the basement. It was beautiful. Mary was in her glory. Some evenings she'd disappear after dinner only to appear again when it was time to go to bed. What she was making was a complete secret.

The Vietnam War continued. Every day, news of death and devastation filled the airwaves. How long would it continue? How many lives would have to be lost before the U.S. would leave that small country? Was it really necessary for our country to be so involved? Nadia wished she could turn on the television and see some good news. Probably not for awhile; the "big guys" said we were there for the duration.

Nadia celebrated her eighteenth birthday on February 12th. It was supposed to be like any other day. Ray and Mary's parents had passed away and there was only one set of aunts and uncles on each side of the family that lived close by. A family party wouldn't attract many people. Jackie, Ginny and Kevin wouldn't be home, so it would only be the three of them. Or so Nadia thought; Ali, Andy and Mary had different ideas. All of Nadia's friends planned to meet at Bemis Hill. They decorated the shelter, started a fire in the huge fireplace, prepared food brought from home, and had everything in its place. When Nadia and her parents arrived, the party would begin.

It turned out to be a beautiful day. Ray, Mary and Nadia decided to take the snowmobiles for a ride on the trails through the woods. It would be a relaxing ride, the thought of which made Mary a little giddy. Nadia suggested that Mary was regressing in her actions, especially when she suggested they take sleds along so they could slide down the hill. It wasn't like Mary. She also carried a brown paper bag with her, protecting it as if it were filled with gold.

"We have to go right now," she insisted. Nadia could not imagine what the hurry was, but she decided to humor her.

The ride was all they imagined it to be, and more. The sun shining on the newly fallen snow made the evergreens glisten. The trees looked like they had been decorated with billions of diamonds. A moose and her two calves were enjoying the beautiful day, nibbling on a cedar tree. They were so engrossed in "lunch" they refused to move off the trail. The family spent a few minutes watching them. Ray was vigilant and alert, however, since these huge animals couldn't be trusted. They were majestic and docile at the moment, but they could charge you for no reason. Just as Ray was pondering how to get around them, the moose ambled back into the forest.

Bemis Hill was bustling with activity when they got there. Nadia couldn't remember ever seeing so many vehicles there at one time. Once the snowmobiles were stopped, they hopped off. Perplexed, Nadia asked where all the people were.

"So many cars, no drivers. Where is everyone?"

She didn't have to wonder long. Forty-some kids came screaming out of the shelter, yelling "Happy Birthday!"

Nadia's friends had pulled off the surprise of the year, much to her obvious delight! When Kevin and Katie came strolling out the door, she could hardly contain herself. The forty plus people there were adults, but today they all acted like kids: sliding down the hill, playing hide and seek in the trees, making snowmen and having snow ball fights. The food disappeared in minutes—everyone was ravenous. It was hard work having so much fun!

Nadia had two gifts to open. (Mary and Ray and all of the parents had an understanding with their kids: when everyone turned thirteen there would be no gifts, just fun get togethers.)

Nadia opened her gift from Katie and Kevin. It was a beautiful backpack in Minnesota's colors, with a smiling gopher engraved on the front and "The University of Minnesota" embossed next to him. Nadia loved it. Little did she know that the backpack would travel many miles with her. Ray and Mary broke the rule a bit and gave her a "Rose of Sharon" pinky ring, the exact one Nadia had paused and stared at many times in the jeweler's window. Friends and family—how could anyone live a day without them, she wondered.

Ray drove home the car Kevin had borrowed from a friend, so Katie could ride on the snocat and see for herself why the Olsons loved snowmobiling so much. She wasn't disappointed. A large buck made an appearance on the trail along with seven or eight rabbits. All agreed that it was the perfect ending to a truly wonderful birthday!

Katie and Kevin went to church with the family. Kevin was very proud when he introduced Katie. Ginny called in the afternoon with the announcement that college was fine but being home would be much better. Nadia reread a card she had received from Jackie a week earlier. Jackie was having a fabulous time. Her host family was great, while the weather was a bit less favorable: rainy, hot and humid. Leeches were prevalent during the monsoon cycles, and Jackie said that it definitely was not cool to be walking through the jungle and find them clinging to your body. She also wrote about a Filipino delicacy, a hard-boiled egg with a duck inside. The markets in the Philippines sold "balot" the way corner stands sell hot dogs in New York.

The next Olson adventure was a trip to the University of Minnesota. They toured the campus and Nadia's dorm. Excitement was building. Nadia was ready to begin the next phase of her life. But she had reservations about leaving her parents. Life would be so different for them; their entire lives had been dedicated to their children. Who would be there to watch the hockey games and baseball games with Ray? Who would help Mary clean house and cook when she was exhausted from teaching? And Buford, who would be there every day to run with him? Each time Nadia voiced these concerns, Mary's answer was always the same: "We'll leave all that in God's hands."

The campus was enormous. How would anyone remember how to get from place to place? Nadia took some pleasure in knowing that thousands of young students had succeeded before her. Surely she would do the same.

Spring was in the air. Baseball spring training had begun in Florida. The NHL was down to its final game before the playoffs began. On the farm, snow was melting at a rapid pace. Patches of soil could be seen in the fields and the cattle were getting restless. The hay was still plentiful but the green pastures were a treat. Ray was engrossed in planning this year's spring planting. Last fall's harvest had been a boost. After several years of average crops, the farm was back in the "green." It certainly made the life of a farmer easier.

Mary and Nadia were in the early stages of planning for graduation at the end of May. Mary was certain that Nadia would be the salutatorian, a feeling that wasn't shared by her daughter. There was a lot of competition. Ali would certainly be high on the list.

Small town, small school, small community—everyone knew everyone else, there could be only one graduation ceremony to be held in the gym and lunch room. This year the mood would be greatly different. The class had lost three of its peers. Never would they be forgotten or ignored. Mary and three other mothers made four inch squares, monogramming them with the names of each senior who had passed away. These would be sewn on the shoulder of each gown. Every senior would carry a red rose, a yellow rose and two stems for ferns. Three enormous balloons had been ordered. The names of each lost student would be printed on them. They would be released at the conclusion of the ceremony.

Buford and Nadia continued running every day. The faithful farm dog would wait patiently by the back door. He knew that at the sound of dishes clattering in the sink, it would only be a few minutes. He and Nadia shared the excitement of spring. Although it hadn't been a harsh winter, it had been a long one, but now the plants and animals were coming out of hibernation. Each day they ran they'd see what kind of vegetation was peeking out of the ground. The crocuses were first: yellow, white and purple filled the gardens. Soon tulips would proclaim their whereabouts, followed by the daffodils. It truly was a time for optimism and anticipation.

Andy was making Nadia's life miserable. He wanted their relationship to be much more than it was—constantly calling her, stopping her in the hall and begging her to accept his class ring, a significant sign to everyone that she was "his girl." Not a chance; he was a true friend but that's all. The last thing Nadia wanted was a boyfriend when she left for college. She wanted to be free, to be able to choose from the vast number of boys that would be available. Andy was not happy with Nadia's choice.

Nadia warned him, "Get over it. If you believe this attitude is worth losing a best friend, keep it up." That was the end of the conversation.

Kevin, Katie and Ginny came home the first weekend in May. Ginny had hitched a ride from Moorhead to Thief River. Having them home made it like old times. The noise level at times was hard on the eardrums.

The spring rains had arrived so the family resigned itself to a day indoors. On Saturday, they started a game of Monopoly in the morning and stopped only for lunch and dinner. Everyone loved it when Katie came. She was still considered company so Mary went all out in the cooking department. As they were sitting down at the table, Kevin smiled and said, "We have an announcement to make. I asked Katie to marry me and she said yes!"

Wow! No one was surprised that he had asked her, but everyone was a little surprised that it had happened this quickly. They must be very much in love. Kevin informed his family that he and Katie were going to finish college next year and get married in June. Katie beamed as she told her "new" family of their plans. They wanted to live on the farm, for a while at least. Kevin would work with Ray and she would get a job at the hospital. They may have only been twenty one years old but they had their future planned. Katie was welcomed with open arms. She would be a perfect addition to the family.

They settled down and enjoyed dinner. "Superb," "splendid," and "magnificent" were words used to describe the venison roast Mary had prepared. She always cooked it until it was almost done and then added potatoes, carrots, onions and her homemade salsa. Keeping the conversation going wasn't a problem. It was obvious that Katie and Kevin had been planning their wedding for quite some time. Katie asked Ginny and Nadia to be bridesmaids. She also wanted Jackie to be a bridesmaid so they planned their wedding around her return date from the Peace Corps. Katie asked Mary if she'd sew her wedding dress.

"I've seen many articles of clothing you have sewn and they are so lovely. Would you think about it?"

Mary quickly replied, "I don't even have to think about it. I would be honored to sew your dress."

A bond between them began at that moment.

Ali and Nadia worked for hours on May baskets. May 1st was a day when you could knock on a door, hang a basket of goodies on the knob and then run before the occupant saw who had left it. This had been an Olson tradition for years. Mary could remember doing it when she was a young girl. Ali thought it was great. Their targets would be mainly the elderly families who were less fortunate and, of course, their friends. Each girl had made twenty baskets. They had sewn 8x8 inch bags and put inside candy, gum, homemade chocolate chip cookies, hot cocoa mix and a homemade card. It took them a few hours to deliver all of them. A feeling of satisfaction was felt between them on the drive home. They were such close friends; everything they did was done as a team. Would college, miles away from one another, allow the friendship to continue?

Spring showed its face everywhere. Leaves were filling the once bare branches; color was exploding in the flower gardens; the lawns were turning a brilliant green; windows were thrown open in homes, allowing the stale air of winter to be blown away; and Ray was working twelve hours a day planting the fields.

Nadia had gotten an excused absence from school to pick up Kevin and Ginny. Everyone was excited about their return home, no one more than Ray. He needed help on the farm.

Ginny had applied for a job at the nursing home. She had an interview the day after returning home. The Director of Nursing had almost guaranteed her a job but he had to go through all the formalities with Ginny. Everything had to be on the up and up or surely someone would complain. Nadia wanted to get a job. Both of her parents pleaded with her to spend one more summer helping on and around the farm. Nadia had to admit the pay was fabulous and the fringe benefits were great. It hadn't taken much persuading before she accepted. She knew there would be plenty of work on the farm.

It took them all day to get Kevin and Ginny moved out of their apartments. It was even more difficult to separate Katie and Kevin. Prior to leaving, they had made a "schedule" when Katie would come to the farm and when Kevin would go to her house. She had gotten a job at the hospital. Work made seeing one another difficult. At last he was in the pickup and the Olsons were on their way home.

Baccalaureate was Sunday evening on May 31st. It was mandatory for all who were graduating to attend. Pastor Jim was in charge of the service. His message gave everyone hope for the future. Throughout the service the classmates who had died were remembered.

The seniors had completed their finals and did not have to attend the last four days of school. Ginny and Nadia finished planting the garden; they mowed the lawn; they cleaned the house; and worked on graduation plans.

The weather was amazing—no rain in the past five days and none was expected in the near future. The guys would be able to complete their spring planting by Friday. Then the rain could fall. The seeds would sprout and soon the black fields would be a brilliant green.

Jackie called on Saturday evening. She was truly enjoying herself. Each day she fell more and more in love with her new Filipino family. She spoke to Nadia, congratulated her and wished her good luck in every aspect of her new life. She talked to Kevin, Ginny, Ray and Mary. Toward the end of the conversation she informed them that she had used up her minutes allowed by Peace Corps. She had one request: "Please send chocolate and two new bras. Address the package to my host mother; otherwise, the chances of me getting the box are slim."

On Sunday morning, Nadia and the graduates were acknowledged in church. Nadia spoke to the congregation on behalf of all the graduates. She had been chosen valedictorian for her class. Her message was short and to the point. "The time has come for us to leave the safety of our parents, to take command of our lives, to continue to live our lives in the way we have been taught. Love God, keep Him close in every endeavor, savor each new experience, learn from our mistakes and (with a grin on her face) always come home whenever possible."

She thanked the congregation and Pastor Jim for their support throughout her growing up years. They would always be a part of her life. She completed her speech and walked directly to her parents.

"I would never have become the young adult I am without your love and concern. Thank you for making God the center of our home and our lives. I love you both with all my heart and will always consider "the farm" my home. God bless both of you."

All of the graduates received a Bible. Pastor Jim asked each of them to read it every day. He said, "Life's trials will be much easier to handle if you keep God close by." On the inside cover was written "I can do all things through Christ who strengthens me." Nadia received dozens of cards from the parishioners. She would open them this evening along with the others she had received in the mail.

The family went directly from church to the school. Gowns, caps and instructions were given to the seniors. At one o'clock sharp they marched into the gym. The entire ceremony was perfect. Andy, who was chosen class salutatorian, spoke first. His speech was written well and delivered enthusiastically. Nadia followed with her speech. Each word she spoke came directly from the heart. Nadia didn't need her notes; she had rehearsed that speech dozens of times.

"Spread your wings, explore the world, make use of every talent given to you. Remain upstanding citizens and always remember your roots. We grew up in a community where love, compassion and friendship abound. Take each of these attributes with you and build a firm foundation wherever life takes you."

Diplomas were handed out and high school was over. Caps flew everywhere, then a moment of silence. The graduates filed out of the gym and released the huge balloons that contained the names of the deceased students and these words: "We will always remember and love you."

On Sunday evening Nadia opened her gifts and cards. Among her favorite gifts was a beautiful watch from her parents. Ginny, Jackie, Kevin and Kate gave her a set of luggage. Nadia was astonished. Where in the world did they get the money to buy a set of Samsonite luggage? She received three sets of towels, a set of bed linen, several photo frames and $590.00. The money was put in her drawer along with the four scholarships she had received. The cost of college was always on her mind. As the summer went by she became less stressed though, because she had saved $1,320.00.

Mary and Nadia had spent hours filling out and sending forms everywhere for any available grants. They knew she'd have to get a student loan, but the smaller the better. Grants and scholarships were free; loans had to be paid back.

It was late before anyone got to bed. Ginny started her new job on Tuesday. Needless to say they slept most of Monday, even Mary! When they did wake up, Kevin and Ray were nowhere in sight. Who had made breakfast for them? The kitchen revealed the answer. Toast on the counter, frying pan with dried eggs, coffee canister sitting open, and a note: "Sorry for the mess. Had to get going. See you at noon."

The women worked in the flower and vegetable garden. The weeds had a way of growing faster and thicker than the plants. They also mowed the lawn. At the end of the day, they were tired but pleased with everything they had accomplished. The family enjoyed a picnic dinner at Bemis Hill. A joke around the community was "We all know when spring has sprung because the Olson family heads to Bemis Hill for their first picnic." Everyone picked the berries of the season during those picnics—strawberries, blueberries, raspberries, or chokecherries. Once they got the fruit home, Mary canned and made pies, jellies and syrups. They were delicious treats in the middle of winter.

The summers go by quickly in northern Minnesota. The Olsons always tried to pack as many fun events in as possible. This year, the Fourth of July brought even more throngs of people to their small town than usual. The planning committee worked hard to entice people to come this year: races for all ages, food stands at the beach, dunking tanks, games, a plate drop with a thousand prizes all donated by local businesses, a parade, and fireworks to conclude the festivities. Kevin drove Andy and Nadia around in a Corvette convertible that Ray had rented. It was hard to tell who was most excited, the homecoming king and queen or the driver. Kevin spit-shined the car and promised he would have it parked in the garage immediately following the parade.

But Ray wouldn't hear of it. "No, that's not necessary. Drive it, enjoy it, and show it off." Kevin did as he was told and probably put more miles on that car than was allowed.

The County Fair followed the Fourth. It was the same size every year, but the older one got, the smaller the fair seemed. Nadia was already beginning to feel this way.

Ray pulled Ginny, Kevin, and Nadia together the day before the fair. "Do you think you kids could keep the homeplace going if I send your mother to the Philippines? I'll be here to help you. I've watched her spend hours writing letters to Jackie. She's very lonesome. What do the three of you think?"

What did they think? Without any hesitation they all spoke at the same time. "We'll work harder than we ever have to make this trip possible for Mom."

That was all it took. At the dinner table that evening, Ray told Mary, "We're all sending you on a trip. You'll be leaving on Monday morning and coming home on the following Wednesday."

Mary was bewildered. "Where am I going and why would you ever want to get rid of me during the busiest time of the year on a farm?"

"You, my dear, are going to see Jackie. No ifs, no protests about us not being able to afford it, no nothing. You are going. The kids and I have already talked it over. We can handle everything."

There were no questions asked. "Thank you, Ray. I miss her so much."

How Ray was able to put all the plans together by himself was a mystery to his children. He laid the itinerary next to Mary's plate. Everyone knew at that point that he had been working on this trip for a long time.

Ginny and Nadia were going to drive Mary to Grand Forks on Sunday. They would stock up on the essentials they felt Jackie needed. Every time she called, the bra topic was brought up. Kevin began calling her "Miss Bra."

It was amazing to all of them how Mary's temperament changed. She was vibrant! She hung lists on the refrigerator. Each day of the week contained jobs to be completed. And each list ended with the same plea: "Be good to one another, help each other, and remember to pray. I love you." It didn't matter to any of them that they would have a few more tasks to do. They knew that Mary and Jackie would have the time of their lives.

Ray and Kevin said goodbye to Mary, and then the women were off to Grand Forks. Mary, Ginny, and Nadia thoroughly enjoyed a day of shopping. Each time one of them saw something they felt Jackie needed, into the shopping cart it went. They also bought a small gift for each member of her Filipino family.

It wasn't difficult for any of them to sleep that night. The alarm rang at 4:00. Showers, a quick stop at the convenience store for coffee and then they were off to the airport. The plane boarded right on time. Nadia ran to her mother. She needed one more hug.

"What if something happens to you? What if I never see you again? Give Jackie many hugs from me. What if the plane crashes? Tell Jackie I love her. Mom, please come home safely."

Mary kept trying to interrupt her, "Oh, of course I'll come home safely. Where is your faith? Go back to Ginny, drive safely home, take care of your Dad, and I'll see you in ten days."

When Nadia turned to Ginny, she found her in the arms of two elderly ladies who were trying to console her. It took all of Nadia's strength to get Ginny into the car. What a mess the two of them were! It was a long, quiet drive home.

The mood was somber at the Olson home that night and the next morning until Mary called just as Nadia was leaving for her morning run. "I'm here, Honey. Everything went well. Jackie and her family were at the airport when I landed. Tell everyone that I love them. Jackie is fine. Once I saw her I wondered why I worried about her so much."Jackie then got on the phone and reassured Nadia that she'd take good care of their mother.

Nadia went to the shed to tell her father the news and then to the Care Center to tell Ginny.

It seemed as though the ten days flew by. Each day they completed the items on their list. Ali, Andy and Katie helped out, as honorary members of the Olson family. If they chose to come to the farm they knew that the chores had to be finished before the fun could start. They must not have minded because they continued to come back.

They did have fun together. Mud running was the big ticket. They found the biggest and muddiest terrain and hit the mud holes at full speed with the four-wheelers. The muddier the riders got, the more fun it was. For all the city slickers in the world, the Olsons had this message: It doesn't get much better than this! When the ride was over, they'd pull the four-wheelers up to the well, pick up the hoses, and spray the machines and the riders until the mud disappeared.

Kevin and Ray's age difference showed up each evening. Baling hay, cultivating the summer fallow, feeding the cattle—it was all in a day's work. Ray was perfectly content to sit back and relax in the evenings. Not Kevin. He'd eat, shower, and then was off to a baseball game, a movie or a game of golf—always joined

by his sisters and Katie. Katie spent every waking moment at the
farm. She'd work her four ten-hour days at the hospital, hop in
the car and spend the next three days at the farm.

Nadia was a natural golfer. Her game drove the guys crazy.
She'd get up to the tee box, hit the ball, walk down the fairway,
hit it again, and walk on to the green to putt. She made it look
so easy. The guys would slice the ball into the water, into the
woods, everywhere except the fairway. Their incompetence drew
laughter from the girls.

Nadia smiled, "Girls rule, boys drool." Golf became the
pastime for the rest of the summer.

Mary was due home on Wednesday. It was difficult to believe
that she had been gone eight days. Everything had gone very
well except for the cooking. They knew Ray was itching to have
some of Mary's mashed potatoes and gravy without lumps. They
had eaten a lot of spaghetti, chili and hot dishes. Ginny and
Nadia knew how to throw a lot of stuff into a pot and cook it.
Ray teased the girls that dinner "filled the empty holes."

On Wednesday morning, they finished haying. Ginny, Kevin
and Ray were leaving at noon to pick up Mary. Kevin planned to
stay in Thief River and get his college courses in order and then
visit Katie and her family. Ginny had transferred to UND this
year, so she needed to go to Grand Forks to make sure everything
was in order for her final year of college. She and Ray would be
at the airport to meet Mary at 6:00. Nadia chose to stay home.
She wanted to finish mowing the lawn and cleaning the house.
Everything had to be perfect for Mary's return. It would be late
before they got home so she, Ali, and Andy played nine holes of
golf.

At 10:00 she saw lights coming down the road and into the
driveway. Elated, she ran out the door and gave her mother a
big, long hug. Mom was home. All of the anxiety, fretting, and
apprehension Nadia had been feeling disappeared. Hundreds of

questions would be asked about Mary's trip, but this moment was spent thanking God for her safe return.

Jackie had written letters to all of them. Mary handed them out along with a gift. At the breakfast table, Mary revealed some interesting facts and tales of her trip.

"The Philippines is a lovely country. People work very hard to make a living. Everyone takes care of one another. Grandparents do not live alone but move in with their children when they can't take care of themselves. It's hot and humid. I used to think it was horrible here during the summer, but nothing could have prepared me for that climate. The sweat poured from morning until night. I can fully understand why clothing doesn't have a long life. The Filipinos love Jackie. Wherever she goes, dozens of children follow. When she speaks, they listen. Her family has very few material possessions, but they have one another and that seems to be enough. Thank you all for this experience. It was wonderful."

Part 2

Another fall was fast approaching. Grain had to be swathed. The combines were pulled from the shed, greased, oiled and gassed up—ready to go. In three weeks an eerie calm would hang over the farm. It would be the first time that all of the kids would be away from home at one time.

During the last week of August, college students started leaving town and returning to school. The Olsons followed their drop off schedule from last year. All three children were packed and ready to go. On Saturday morning Kevin was the first to leave with a short goodbye. Ray kept reminding the rest of all the miles that had to be driven. They proceeded on to Grand Forks where they moved Ginny in.

They arrived in Minneapolis at the University of Minnesota late that afternoon. Nadia was excited but she wasn't prepared for the mass confusion and utter chaos! Hundreds of cars, pickups and trailers were all trying to park and unload. She found that it was no better inside the dorm. It's hard to imagine nine beds being carried up the stairs one after the other! Nadia thought that some of the fathers who were helping should have stayed in their vehicles so the rest of the people wouldn't have to listen to their foul language.

Nadia's room was on the second floor, the first one by the door. Ray, Mary and Nadia carried up the bed, a small dresser, television, clothes and two boxes of goodies. Packed neatly were jams, jellies, sauce, salsa, cookies, bread and bars. The luggage was last; it weighed a ton. Once everything was in the room Nadia suggested that her parents get on the road because it was already 8:00. Ray had promised the kids they would stay overnight in a motel if it was necessary. Their uncertainty in leaving Nadia was clear. Ray and Mary were both talking at once.

"Lock your door all of the time, don't go out after dark, don't trust anyone, be sure to eat, and don't forget to pray."

Nadia followed them to their car. The scene when they left was duplicated all along the street: goodbyes, hugs and tears. She watched her parents until their pickup disappeared.

In this vast, seemingly unyielding place Nadia would call home for the next four years, fright, terror and panic overcame her. She walked to her room, lay down on the unmade bed and cried herself to sleep. She awoke to the sound of a bell ringing. Confused and startled for a moment, she forgot where she was. The sounds were coming from the bell tower at the church on the corner. She was amazed to find that she had slept twelve hours. When had she ever slept that long? She hadn't heard from her parents so they must have made it home safely.

Her first day at college and her first stab at independence! She was excited to decorate her room. It was small but it was hers. She first placed the log cabin quilt and the matching pillow sham on her bed. In doing so, she could feel Mary's presence and Nadia felt comforted. She hung up her clothes, the shower curtain and three pictures. Her room was already looking like home. A beautiful 8 x 10 picture of her family found its place on her desk. Ray had given her an aerial picture of the farm. On the back was written: "Just don't want you to forget your roots! Love, Dad." At that moment she wished she could be twelve again. She whispered to herself, " I love you too, Mom and Dad. Thank you for the best life any child could ever ask for."

She had time for a quick shower. She wanted to get to the bank and open a checking account. She had $900 stashed in the cookie jar—not exactly the safest place to keep your life's savings! She stopped at the convenience store on her way home and got a small pizza and pop. The hunger pains were ghastly and the growling coming from her stomach was embarrassing.

Elaine, the housemother, was delightful. It was not difficult to figure out why she'd held onto this job for twenty-some years. She knew everything. Years ago they nicknamed her "Mrs. Encyclopedia" and the name stuck. She handed Nadia every bus schedule available, a detailed map for anyone who ran or walked, a menu for the next week, a list of Nadia's classes—including the professors' names—a list of cab companies (assuming that a college student would be able to afford a cab in emergencies anyway). Nadia brought all of the information to her room. As she walked in she was talking to herself. There was so much to learn and remember. "You can do this, farm girl," she convinced herself.

It was 5:00 and she was exhausted. Maybe a quick run would wake her up. She grabbed the map. Where was Buford? Who would she tell all her secrets to? Nadia ended up running five miles. She had to double track because she was a little confused about which way to turn at one point. The run took her through the campus and she even recognized the names on some of the buildings. Sweating and tired, she was glad to be back in the lobby of her dorm. There were students all over the place, greeting one another with a brief "Hi" or "How are you?" She had no major conversations with anyone though—maybe tomorrow. As she was climbing the stairs, Elaine stopped her. "Your parents called. Maybe you should call them back." With a wink and a smile she was gone. Little did Nadia know what a wonderful friend and mother figure Elaine would become.

Nadia called home collect. She heard Mary accept the charges.

"Hi, Honey! Dad and I miss you and are so lonesome. There is nothing wrong; we just wanted to hear your voice. Buford misses you even more. He sits by the door for hours. I suppose Dad and I will have to take up walking."

She had helped Ray haul grain to the elevator. The weather was beautiful: low 70s and no wind. The hired man would stay until October first, at which time he had to report to a job in Illinois.

"That's about all the news I have. How about you?"

Nadia blinked back the tears and tried to sound happy and positive. Before the call was completed she almost broke down though. Ray joined the conversation on the phone in the bedroom. He had Nadia laughing with his stories—some true, all true, none true—who knows, but it worked.

Nadia reminded them to take care of Buford. "Tell him I love him and miss him. I'll call you guys on Friday."

The Twins were playing at home. She watched the last four innings. They beat the Boston Red Sox 9—3. She wondered when she'd have time to attend her first game. Her class schedule was tough. She heard that the professors took it easy the first week—not much homework—but she had been warned that it wouldn't last.

On Saturday at noon Nadia walked to the bus stop and boarded A5 for downtown. Less than fifteen minutes later she stood gazing at the mammoth dome. A queasy feeling settled in her stomach. How long had she waited to watch a major league baseball game? She dug in her pants pocket and took out a five-dollar bill and her ID card. Nadia passed the money and card under the window. A crabby, obviously irritated man glared at her.

"Don't you realize they are playing the White Sox? The game is sold out."

With that, he turned around on his stool and continued his conversation with his co-workers. Nadia slowly turned around, tears flowing, and headed toward the bus stop.

"Miss, what's wrong?" An elderly couple walked up to her.

"It doesn't matter," she said and kept walking. The lady touched her shoulder. "We have an extra ticket for the game. Would you like to join us?"

"Thank you, but I only have $5.00 because I thought that college students could get in for a dollar."

"Just follow us and it won't cost you a penny." The lady took Nadia's arm.

As they walked into the dome, Nadia's stomach started churning. She thought she was going to throw up. This place was even bigger than she had imagined. And the people—thousands of them milling around! The game wouldn't start for another hour and a half. The elderly couple waited patiently while Nadia stood and soaked it all in. It was as if they knew how she was feeling. They put her in between them as they started on the journey to their seats. Down they went, row after row of seats, which brought them closer and closer to the field. Nadia's heart was beating so hard it felt as though it would leave her body. There were no more steps. She found herself sitting in the front row! Right in front of them the Twins were stretching, bending, throwing and batting. Nadia found herself almost in a frenzy! This is not what she expected in her first trip to watch the Twins. Not a word was spoken. The couple allowed her to savor every moment.

"Do you have a camera with you?" the man asked.

"No, I thought I'd be sitting in the nosebleed section. The players would have looked like ants."

"We'll take lots of pictures and send them to you."

Pen in hand, they wrote down Nadia's address. The players must have been ready for the game. The field emptied and the crew appeared out of nowhere; raking, adjusting bases, touching up the foul lines. Even that impressed Nadia.

The gentleman ordered three sodas, two bags of popcorn, and a bag of sunflower seeds. He offered popcorn and a soda to Nadia.

Introductions were made. His name was Sal and his wife's name was Sandy. He was the president of a large corporation in Minneapolis. The reason they had three tickets was because of their grandson who had always attended games with them, but couldn't this time because he had just left for Harvard University. Deep in her heart, Nadia hoped he never came home.

Pandemonium erupted as the Twins ran out on the field. Sal leaned over to talk to a player. Nadia sneaked a glance. What she saw was the most gorgeous man she had ever met—black hair, beautiful smile showing off white teeth, perfect body and a deep voice.

Sal turned to her. "Nadia, I'd like you to meet Nate. He's our catcher."

Nadia managed a weak "hello." She knew who he was and everything about him. He was her hero, her favorite Twins player, her "dream man." He smiled. Her heart pounded.

"Sal, wait a few minutes after the game and we'll take pictures," Nate said.

Nadia pinched herself. Was this a dream? Was someone playing a trick on her? She dared not close her eyes for fear that reality would set in.

It was a nail biter of a game. The Twins scored first on a home run from Racus. Back and forth it went. At the top of the ninth, the score was 5-5. The Twins held off the White Sox with three quick outs. Then it was the top of the order for the Twins. There was a first out with a pop up fly to second base, then a second out with a ground ball to the shortstop. Nadia could hardly look. When she did, she saw that Nate was up—one strike, two strikes, third pitch thrown; he swings and the crowd goes wild. Home run—the game was over!

Sal and Sandy watched Nadia. The excitement in her voice, cheering, jumping—her total elation—made them feel young again.

True to his word, Nate made his way over to them. Sal offered congratulations. "Great game, great hit—couldn't have come at a better time."

"Thanks," replied Nate, "are you ready for a picture?" He was looking directly at Nadia. "I didn't know you and Sandy had a granddaughter."

Laughing, Sal introduced Nadia. "This is Nadia Olson, our new friend. We met her in front of the dome just as she was leaving. We would gladly adopt her."

They took several pictures and then Nate said, "Let's get one with Nadia and myself. Ready?"

"Okay" was all she could squeak out. Nate motioned for her to come closer. He put his arm around her waist. Nadia fainted. When she came to, she was sitting in the dugout with people all around. Embarrassed, she started crying.

"Please, I just want to go home."

Sal, Sandy, and Nate tried to console her to no avail. She ran up the stairs, out the door and continued to run the eighteen blocks to her dorm. Why, why, why did she allow that to happen? The one picture she wanted so badly was the one she wouldn't receive. She decided to go to bed and hope that everything would be better in the morning.

At six o'clock she was wide awake. She stretched, got up and made her bed. Hunger pains ran through her body. She realized the only thing she had eaten was a little popcorn. Nadia knew that she had shed a few more pounds since she had moved, and it probably wasn't a good thing.

As Nadia walked to the shower she noticed a paper by the door. She must have slept so hard that she never heard the knock on her door. The note read: "Sal, Sandy and Nate were here to see you. Please call them when you wake up." The phone numbers were written on the bottom. First thought: I'll throw it, rip it up, get rid of it, never to be embarrassed again. Instead, she folded it and laid it on the desk.

The shower felt great. Nadia allowed the water to pelt her. She chose jeans and a red t-shirt. She would go for a run and check out the churches close to the dorm. She had breakfast, consisting of a bagel, orange juice and a banana. It wasn't Mary's Sunday morning breakfast, but it filled the empty spots.

Nadia's first class on Monday morning was "Introduction to Psychology." The professor was exciting and energizing. There were eighty students in the class. The professor told them about the competition in this field. He said that forty percent of them would change their majors before graduation. Nadia vowed that she would be in the sixty percent that would graduate with a psychology major. She would study hard and stick with it.

The length of time between classes was just long enough to grab a bite to eat: yogurt and a BLT. The majority of students were surprised at the amount of homework they received. Nadia spent at least four hours a night at the library. The weeks and months flew by. Then semester exams were right around the corner. The phone calls home were the highlight of the week. Ginny, Kevin and Katie would all be home for Thanksgiving. Nadia was catching a ride to Duluth and then riding home with Ali.

Two more notes had been delivered to her. Both of them were from Sal and Sandy. One contained pictures they had taken at the baseball game.

"Nadia, we know you are extremely busy. We are leaving for Florida this weekend. Please call us. We'd love to see you before we leave."

The pictures were fabulous. They even managed to get one with Nadia and Nate standing next to one another with four other players. Embarrassment quickly crept back. She wanted to call them but how could she face them after acting like a total idiot at the game? She made a rational decision: She'd swallow her pride and make the call. Hopefully, there wouldn't be many students in the lobby just in case she started to cry. Heaven knows they'd seen her cry more often than necessary. Maybe Sandy and Sal wouldn't be home and she could leave a message.

No such luck. Sandy answered the phone. "Hi, Nadia, we were afraid we'd miss you."

The conversation flowed. Sandy was very easy to talk to. "We're flying out tomorrow morning. Would you have time for dinner tonight?"

They told her they would pick her up at 6:00. Nadia took great care in getting ready. Exactly at 6:00 their white Cadillac pulled up and both of them got out. Sandy looked lovely in a brown suit with a tan shirt and tan heels. No matter what Nadia had put on, she would have felt underdressed. They had dinner at Jax. She told them she had a lot of work to do, so they dropped her off at the dorm right after dinner. Before she got out of the car, Sal asked if she'd like to join them in the Bahamas for spring break.

Nadia was taken completely off guard. "What did you say, Sal?"

He repeated the question. Nadia, as usual, stumbled for words. She finally managed to say, "Oh, thanks for the invitation but I don't know if I can go. My Mom's not feeling well."

Sal told her to think about it. " You have lots of time before you have to make a decision."

Nadia got out of the car and looked at both Sandy and Sal. "Thank you for everything. Have a good winter and think about us here in Minnesota when it's twenty below zero. Write if you have time." They assured her that she would receive many letters. Nadia gave them each a hug and walked away.

It took Nadia until 11:00 to finish her homework. Just as she was falling asleep a thought came to her: Sandy and Sal hadn't mentioned Nate's name once. She supposed he was doing what all professional sports players did in their off season—vacationing, golfing somewhere in the warm south, skiing in the Alps—having a lot of fun.

The next morning, Nadia was going over her plan. She had to take two tests today and two more tomorrow, and then she would be off for four days. She could hardly wait to go home; the anticipation was almost too much for her to concentrate on school work.

That afternoon, Nadia decided to go for a run before studying. She was doing stretches when she heard her name. Turning around she saw Nate. Of course, no quick greeting came to her, and she was frustrated: Why was she able to speak fluently around other people but not Nate?

He asked, "Do you mind if I join you on your run?"

"Yes, I mean no, sure you can," Nadia was thinking that this was going to be an interesting forty minutes.

"I've been here ten times hoping I'd catch you. You must have a different class schedule every day."

"Yup, as soon as I'm done, I run. I know that if I sit down I'll probably not have enough energy to get up." Nadia actually found herself relaxing in Nate's presence. "You had a great season. Player of the year—that's quite an accomplishment, especially in your second full year in the majors."

"Yea, it was very nice." Conversation became easy, especially when they started talking about Sal and Sandy. Nate explained that they were part owners of the team.

"Sal and the rest of the owners have a big undertaking this winter. They want to sign the first baseman, two pitchers, and two outfielders, all for five-year contracts. I don't think it will be a problem except for Joe, who has his heart set on the Yankees. You know, with the Yankees' bank roll, they'll be able to offer him just about anything. The owners and the management feel that next year is the Twins' golden year. If they can keep the team together we'll have a good shot at winning the World Series."

The conversation turned to Nadia. Where is she from, what major is she choosing, how old is she, how many brothers and sisters does she have—so many questions but Nadia didn't mind answering them. The forty minutes flew by. As they neared the dorm he asked her if she'd like to go for a pizza.

"Absolutely!" This time, Nadia was quick to respond. "Fair warning though, I'm starved."

She ran up to her room, changed her shirt and pants, sprayed on a little perfume and left the dorm. They drove to Pizza Palace, ordered a large taco pizza and ate the whole thing. Nate told her about his family. Both of his parents were doctors and, except for a sister who was studying in London, his family lived in Sioux Falls, South Dakota. All of them were avid golfers (that brought a smile to Nadia's face), and they put a lot of effort into spending time as a family, although that was getting to be more difficult. His mother gave hours and hours of her time to community service. They were Lutherans and, yes, they went to church.

"Dad always told both of us kids that he couldn't control what we did every minute of our lives, but he could expect us to be in church on Sunday morning. Still today, every conversation I have with Mom ends the same way: "Love you, don't forget to pray, go to church and do one thing every day to make someone else's life better and happier."

Did that statement ever sound familiar! Nadia looked around to see if Mary had sneaked into the building.

It was nearing 9:00. She explained that her homework was waiting for her. On the way home, Nate asked if he could see her again.

Nadia was shocked at how quickly she answered. Nate was even more shocked at the answer.

"No, I think it would be better if you just remained my baseball idol and friend. This could never work. I'm a poor college student from a farm in the sticks of northern Minnesota. You are a baseball player, good-looking and rich. You have traveled all over the world, I have never been outside of Minnesota. I know what my feelings are for you. I could fall in love this minute, but I don't want to get hurt and inevitably it would happen. I am perfectly happy to have met you, and I can tell my family and friends . . ."

He didn't let her finish. "Your perception of me is very wrong. I put my jeans on the same way you do. I work my ass off every day for six or seven months. I travel to different cities to play baseball, not to see which girl I can pick up. Who cares if I'm a baseball player and you're a farm girl? I like you; you're fun to be with; and you're beautiful, intelligent and ambitious."

"Thank you, Nate, but I won't change my mind." Nadia exited the car. Nate caught up with her. "I wish you'd give me a chance. We could have many good times together."

It was too late; Nadia was through the door. She thought, "I must be crazy to let a man like that get away."

It seemed as though the entire lobby was filled with students staring at her. At least she wasn't crying. Upstairs in her room she kept analyzing the situation. Maybe she had read too many articles and had heard too many stories about the lives of professional sports players. Well, it was too late to have second thoughts now.

Nadia did some late night cramming for her tests. Her ride was leaving immediately after her class tomorrow, so she packed her suitcase before she went to bed.

The tests were easy. She knew every answer and felt satisfied as she waited for Brian. It was a quiet ride. Brian never spoke unless she asked him a question. Thankfully the ride was only two hours long. The second half of the ride was wonderful though. She and Ali caught each other up on all the gossip. Three months was a long time to be separated from your best friend. The girls chatted about classes, schedules, boys, dorms, weird students, holidays and home. Nadia never said a word about Nate. Before they realized it, Ali was honking the horn while driving down the Olson driveway. Ray, Mary, Ginny, Kevin and Katie all ran out the door. For a split second she wondered where Jackie was. She had been very faithful in writing to Jackie every week. It was always good to hear back from her, but Nadia was missing her more each day and there was still another year to go.

The car had barely come to a stop and Nadia was out—hugging everyone. "Where's Buford?" she asked. At that very moment he came barreling around the corner.

Someone in the crowd said, "Well, we know now who rates the highest in this home!"

Homecomings were the greatest. The Olsons had four days to be together and Nadia enjoyed every one of them.

The ground was completely bare. No snow meant the activity itinerary had to be changed, because there would be no snocatting. Mary had Off-da tacos for dinner that night. Everyone helped clean up the kitchen so they could start playing Monopoly, the Olsons' favorite winter game. At 1:45 in the morning they were still deep into the game. Ray stood up, proclaimed himself the winner, and told the rest that it was time to go to bed.

Thanksgiving Day started at 8:00 with a call from Jackie. Everyone got to visit with her. She reminded them that Thanksgiving was just another day in the Philippines, so it was work as usual. She was extremely happy with the success her students were showing in reading. It was obvious from the conversation that Jackie was concerned about Christmas; never had she been apart from her family on that day. Every Peace Corps volunteer was told that he or she could take a few days off, but the expense of flying home made the trip impossible for Jackie. Ray and Mary had offered many times to pay for her ticket but she flatly refused. At the end of the conversation, they all reluctantly said goodbye, realizing that Jackie's return was still a long time away.

Soon after the phone call ended, Katie had an idea. "Let's get pictures of everything, starting with Jackie flying out of Grand Forks. We'll make an album and send it to her. Each of us can write something about an event."

Even Ray, who wasn't much on writing, enjoyed working on the project. Mary was excused. She had to stuff the turkey, put the pies together and finish making lefse. Everyone else pitched in, and the album turned out to be beautiful. They decided to keep it and add pictures from Christmas.

wOnce they sat down to Mary's dinner, her panic subsided. The meal was delicious. In half an hour the Olsons had consumed enough food to feed an army. Kevin admitted to eating nine pieces of lefse plus double helpings of everything else. They pretty much cleaned up every bowl, except for the cranberries, which no one liked, except Mary who insisted that cranberries provided much-needed color. Once again, Mary had outdone herself, and to show their appreciation, everyone else cleaned up the kitchen. They spent the rest of the evening watching football and relaxing.

Accepting the fact that they were no different from thousands of other Americans, the Olsons took off for Grand Forks to do a little shopping on Friday. It was a zoo in every store. There were lines of people checking out at Target and WalMart. Kevin and Ray managed to keep their sanity by dropping the women off and going to the Arctic Cat dealership, a farm store and Menard's—any place they could spend time and not be stampeded.

The four women did a great job of spending money. They enjoyed one another's company even when they had to spend time in check-out lanes. Jackie was always on their minds. Every time they'd see something she might enjoy or need they bought it. The day ended with dinner at Applebee's and then it was time to go home.

The ride home was torture for all of the riders who tried to stay awake. At one point, Ray let out a holler, "Someone has to wake up and talk to me. You have a choice, wake up or we'll all be sleeping permanently!" That got everyone's attention, and the car was filled with chatter until they got home.

They awoke to see the snow falling. It must have snowed all night because the ground was covered in four inches. The accumulation was not quite enough to take the snowmobiles out to get Christmas trees, however, so they'd have to use the four-wheelers. They set out at 10:00. Again, it was a family occasion: Mary rode inside the sled and the rest all found their places. They had hundreds of trees to choose from on the north forty. The Olson family Christmas trees had to be perfect. After examining dozens, they settled on a Norway pine and a spruce. Nadia checked her watch. It had taken them only two and a half hours to make their selections—record time!

Kevin and Ray set the Christmas trees up in the living room and family room downstairs. After lunch, they began the task of decorating. They decided to decorate the tree in the family room first with the homemade kids' decorations that Mary had saved over the years. The memories and stories those elementary school decorations conjured up were wonderful. It always took twice the time to decorate that tree as it did to decorate the one upstairs, which consisted of elegant and carefully-chosen ornaments. This year it was clear lights with red balls, red poinsettias and white doves. When they plugged in the lights and surveyed the final result, everyone agreed that the view was breathtaking.

Andy stopped by for the third time that day. Mary asked him to take some family pictures so she could send them to Jackie. The day was spent wrapping presents, decorating Christmas cookies and writing Christmas cards. On Sunday morning they went to the early church service. Then Nadia and Ali left for Duluth where Nadia would catch her ride to Minneapolis. It wasn't so difficult to leave this time, because Christmas was only three weeks away. Once in Ali's car, Nadia realized she had not said a word about Nate.

Upon returning to her dorm, the house mother stopped her with the news that Nadia had two packages and three letters.

Nadia put her suitcase and bag filled with goodies from Mary on the bed and opened the financial statement from the University. She couldn't take her eyes off the paper because it said that she had a credit balance of $40,000. She lived from day to day so how could she possibly have that much money! It was surely some mistake, and she would have to pay a visit to the financial office tomorrow.

She picked up another envelope. It was a card from Sal and Sandy, wishing her and her family a Happy Thanksgiving and letting her know that all was well. Sal and Sandy and their family had flown down for the holidays and they were waiting to hear if she had made a decision about spring break. They said they missed her contagious laugh.

The third envelope contained a Thanksgiving card from Nate. He hoped she'd had a great time at home and that there had been plenty of snow for snocatting. He was home with his parents and wanted to know if he could call her. He signed the card "A friend always, Nate." Nadia smiled.

She opened the first package from Sal and Sandy. Inside was a beautiful red, white and blue sweater with a matching turtleneck. Nadia tried them on. They fit perfectly. The second package was from Nate. Nadia saw the note first: "Nadia, I got this for you so you can keep in touch with your family and friends. Overseas minutes are included so you can call your sister in the Philippines. Of course, I had my own interest in mind; I'd like to keep in touch with you. You'll receive the bills, so no one else will see who you're calling. I've paid for this plan for thirty-six months. Enjoy it and use it, or it will be a waste of money. Have a good three weeks before Christmas break. Nate."

Her first thought was to close the box and send it back, but she changed her mind when she realized how nice it would be to call home whenever she wanted to—and talk to Ali, Jackie, Ginny, Kevin, Katie and anyone else who came to mind. She took the phone out of the box, plugged it in and proceeded to unpack. She wanted to get to bed early to try and catch up on lost sleep. The second her head hit the pillow, she was asleep.

Nadia called home at 7:00 a.m. They were surprised to hear her voice. She didn't tell them about the phone. It would mean she would have to explain the entire situation. "I just wanted to thank you for the wonderful weekend. I love you, Mom and Dad."

When she left the dorm for the Financial Aid Office, snow was falling, and the world was truly beautiful. She gave her name and ID number to the receptionist, who looked up at her.

"What can I help you with?"

Nadia gave her the letter. "There has to be a mistake here. I only wish I had that much money."

The receptionist did a little checking and returned. "There is no mistake. A deposit was made to your account the day before Thanksgiving."

"Where did the money come from?"

"Sorry, Nadia, I am not able to give out that information. You can make an appointment and speak to one of the advisors."

Nadia left the office more confused than when she walked in. Who was it? Sal, Sandy, or Nate—no one else she knew had money like that. She glanced at her watch. Five minutes to get to class! She ran, hoping to be only a little late.

There were only three weeks of classes left before Christmas break, but Nadia thought that the professors' expectations of the students were ridiculous. She spent hours and hours in the library along with dozens of other students. She finished a paper for Psychology, which she still had to type. Writing was never a problem for Nadia, but she hated typing. What she really wanted to do was write to Jackie but her eyes wouldn't stay open. She decided she would sleep a few hours in the hope that she would awaken feeling refreshed and inspired.

When she returned to her room, Nadia discovered that Ginny had left a message. She called her sister immediately.

"Ginny, what's up?"

"I'm sick of doing homework so I took a break and called you."

"Same here!"

Nadia broke down and told her sister about Nate. At the end of the lengthy conversation, Ginny said, "You goofball, date him. He sounds like a keeper to me."

"Right—for me and thirty other girls around the country. You don't really think he picked me out of the crowd and doesn't do the same in New York, Chicago—wherever he is playing ball."

"Maybe he does, but I still think you should give him a chance."

Nadia had just gotten her pajamas on when the phone rang. It was Nate.

"Hi Nadia. How was Thanksgiving?"

"It was great. What are you doing?"

"I'm flying in tomorrow for a meeting about my contract, which has to be renewed this year. Would you have dinner with me?"

"I'd love to, but I'm loaded down with homework."

"Please Nadia, I really need to talk to you. We can make it a fast food meal to save time." She agreed to meet him at McDonalds.

The next morning, Nadia gave a presentation in one of her classes and was relieved to find out that she had gotten an A. This news put her in a good mood, so she was ready and waiting for Nate when he showed up at her dorm at 8:00. There was only one problem: She was in jeans and a sweatshirt and he in a suit and tie. Nadia was ready to run back inside to change, but Nate jumped out of the car with jeans in hand and asked if he could change in the first floor bathroom. Nadia appreciated his sense of humor but told him that he looked great and should keep his suit on.

They drove though McDonalds and ordered Big Macs and chocolate shakes, which they ate while sitting in their parked car. Conversation was so easy between them. Nate never seemed to run out of things to say about any topic: religion, politics, and family—even women's weight and age. Nadia forgot about the time and how tired she felt earlier in the evening. All of the school work she had to do could wait; she loved being with Nate.

Suddenly the conversation turned serious. Nate asked if she had missed him, and Nadia wondered how she was going to answer the question without lying.

"Nadia, I have to make a decision about my contract by the end of the week. Do I want to sign with the Twins for another four years? Absolutely I do, but there is a problem: Nadia, I like you very much. No, I love you. I think about you all of the time. I need you to be truthful with me. Do you have any feelings for me whatsoever?"

Nadia was thinking about the conversation she had had with Ginny earlier. She wanted to give Nate a chance, but couldn't quite believe that he was sincere. Before she could respond, Nate spoke again. "I have some options, such as signing with the Dodgers, which would give me a whole lot more money. But I don't want to leave you."

"I don't know what to say, Nate. I'm too young and scared to make a decision like that. But I do know one thing: You should definitely stay with the Twins. How could you even think of going to a different team? The Twins have been rebuilding for two years and they are finally in contention for a World Series win, and you are the main force on the team." She took a deep breath and then continued. "I'm so happy when you call. I'm envied by the girls in the dorm each time you pick me up. I'm proud to be seen with you. We laugh and have fun when we are together, but I can't tell anyone you are my 'boyfriend.' What if two weeks from now a picture of you and another girl appears in the paper with the caption: 'Most eligible bachelor takes the leap.' It's easy for you to like me and go on your way, but it's difficult for me to see you leave week after week, spending the next few days partying and playing ball. Don't take me for a fool, Nate. I read every magazine and sports article in the newspapers. I know how you guys live."

"Are you finished, Nadia? Not everyone is like that. The only caption you'll read about me taking the leap is if you are in the picture with me. You only have to answer one question—no more babbling. Do you have feelings for me and do I have a chance at being a part of your life. Yes or no?"

"No, we are too different."

"Okay, Nadia, no more talking. Take care of yourself and study hard. I know you'll do well and be a success in whatever you do. I love you and probably always will. You know what they say about a first love."

Nadia watched him drive away while walking slowly to the dorm. She should have been feeling relieved, having made a tough decision. The truth was that she had a sinking feeling that she had make a mistake. Thank goodness, Christmas vacation was only a week away. She couldn't wait to see her mother.

Nadia took the city bus to Southgate Mall the next day. She wanted to do a little shopping for her family and for Sal and Sandy. Her family was easy, but what do you buy for someone who has everything? She settled on a pewter frame and a coffee mug with "Sal" engraved on it. She wrapped the frame and mug as soon as she got back to the dorm and took the package to the post office.

The next week went by quickly. Nadia's arrangements for going home were exactly the same as Thanksgiving. The day she was leaving she got a package from Sal and Sandy: a sweatshirt and leggings and a gift card to Target. There was also a note: "We are very excited to have you join us for spring break. We bought your plane ticket and will send it to you in February.

Hope school is going well. We were disappointed to hear about you and Nate, and we hope that you will rethink your decision. He is a very sad young man. Have a great Christmas with your family. Love from both of us."

Part 3

Christmas vacation was wonderful: no worries, no homework, no decisions to make—just good food, lots of laughter and sleep, visits with friends, snocatting, and running with Buford and family. Time flew by. New Years Eve came and went; the night had never been a big deal for Nadia. She, Ginny, Kevin, and Katie went to a party at Andy's. It was quite boring but they stayed until midnight and went home to play a few games of gin rummy.

Nadia wondered what Nate was doing, but as soon as the thought crossed her mind, she realized that it was silly to think about him. She was the one who sent him away.

This time Nadia shed tears as they drove away from the farm. It would be three months before she'd be home for Easter. At that moment she hated college. She didn't like the boy she rode with to Minneapolis; she didn't have a good friend like Ali at school; and there was really nothing to look forward to. When she walked into the dorm, however, the familiar activity and chatter made her feel a little more at home.

Nadia picked up her mail: the schedule for her second semester, a card from Jackie, a letter from the church she had been attending, and another from a sorority. She was bored, so bored she brought a book to the lobby in hopes she would find someone to visit with. No such luck, so she went back up the stairs to her room. She might as well go to bed—so much for the exciting college life. She dared not call home. The tears were too close and a phone call to her family would only make things worse.

Nadia made a countdown calendar for spring break. Each day her feet got colder and colder. She didn't really want to go to the Bahamas, but Sal and Sandy had spent hundreds of dollars on her ticket and motel room. She had made a commitment. There was no turning back.

Time flew by. Nadia was enjoying her classes, especially the Psychology class with a very inspiring professor. He was personable and constantly reminded his students that it hadn't been so long since he had been in their shoes.

Nadia called home the night before she left. Mary encouraged her to have fun and take advantage of this special opportunity. She said that she and Ray had a surprise waiting for her when she returned.

It was ten below zero when she boarded the plane in Minneapolis and 72 degrees when she landed in Miami. Sal and Sandy were there to greet her. They had two hours until their flight to the Bahamas. Nadia wanted to go outside and feel the warmth; she couldn't get enough. At that moment, she couldn't imagine ever living in a climate with wintry conditions again.

The flight to the Bahamas was fun. The mood of the passengers was totally different from the one she sensed on the domestic flight. It was easy to tell that everyone was on vacation and happy to get away from the hustle and bustle of everyday life for a while. Tropical drinks were served to the passengers as fast as they could drink them. Nadia noticed that Sal and Sandy were drinking water with lemon, so she ordered the same thing. Having just turned twenty in February, Nadia wondered when she would have her first taste of alcohol.

If she was taken with the weather in Miami, she was exuberant over the experience when she stepped out of the plane: blue skies—not a cloud to be seen—and 82 warm luscious degrees and a slight breeze, just enough to make the palm trees sway. It was heaven on earth! The local people treated the Americans like royalty. Their hotel was right next to the ocean, complete with a fourth floor view, huge deck, and every amenity imaginable. Nadia had her own room. She was excited about spending six days and seven nights in complete luxury, something that she had never before experienced.

Sal gave her an itinerary. "This isn't cut in stone," he said. "We can make changes and substitutions. Our goal is to make sure you enjoy yourself."

"I don't think that will be a problem. I could easily spend the next six days just sitting by the ocean."

The resort was all-inclusive. Nadia was given a card to use for anything she needed. She never knew if this was true or not, but Sal told her that whatever wasn't spent on her card would go back to the hotel. Well, the hotel wouldn't get anything back from her, as she had no trouble spending money.

Nadia was on her way to the beach when she heard a familiar "Hey!" When she turned around, she almost collided with Nate. His appearance took her by complete surprise.

"What are you doing here?"

"Our family comes here every year for a few days before my season begins."

Nate quickly offered the information that he wasn't there at the behest of Sal and Sandy. And when Nadia asked him if he knew she was going to be there, he just as quickly denied the assertion and acknowledged that meeting her was a complete surprise.

Just then a beautiful girl came running up to him. "Nate, is this Nadia?"

For some reason, Nadia found it difficult to believe that he didn't know she was going to be there. But she stood by while he made the introductions. "Hi, Carrie, yes this is Nadia. Nadia, this is my sister Carrie."

Carrie's warm handshake made Nadia feel an immediate liking for Nate's sister. When Carrie said that she had heard so much about Nadia and then asked her if she had come with Sal and Sandy, Nadia looked at Nate and started laughing, "You did know that I would be here. It's nice to meet you, Carrie. You look exactly like your brother. Yes, I came with Sal and Sandy and I have to say that I'm enjoying every minute of my decision to come. Being from Minnesota where the temperature is at this very moment below zero, I think of this as paradise!"

Nate was standing between them, his body language proving that he was one happy man to be in the presence of two pretty women. As the conversation continued, however, he became a little dismayed. He was left standing alone as Nadia and Carrie walked away and got settled on the beach, already talking as if they had known each other forever. Nate sauntered over and asked if he could join them. They invited him to sit down, but he was never able to really join in the conversation.

After a couple of hours, four adults joined them. Sal looked at Nadia, "Hey, here you are. We were a little worried about you."

Nadia smiled, "I found a new friend. I was wondering if it would be okay for us to go into the city tonight."

"Absolutely," Sal glanced at Nate. "Is he going with you?

"He can come with us if he wants to." Nadia was reluctant to give Nate the message that all was okay with her. Besides, she still wasn't convinced that he hadn't followed her.

Sandy cleared her throat and introduced the two strangers. "Nadia, these are Carrie and Nate's parents, Tom and Elaine."

Now Nadia definitely believed that she was part of a conspiracy. "It's nice to meet you."

The four adults sat down in the cabana while the younger three kept visiting. At four o'clock they asked to be excused so they could take showers and get ready for the evening. Nadia needed to know that Sal and Sandy weren't upset by her plans, and Sal assured her that they wanted her to have a good time.

The night turned out to be interesting. They went to a nightclub called "Beach Bash" and found the place to be packed and noisy. Nadia was intrigued by her new experience. Nate, however, was finding it too hard to keep the inebriated vultures away from his companions, so they didn't stay long. Carrie and Nadia went along with his decision to leave.

The three of them walked along the beach to the hotel. It was only midnight, too early to go to bed. They could hear music as they entered the lobby. The band was fantastic, and the three of them had a good time dancing—until other guys asked Nadia to dance. Nate was obviously jealous, and Carrie felt it necessary to straighten him out. "Unless you're married, don't try to tell her what to do."

In all honesty, Nadia would have preferred to dance with Nate all night, but the band quit playing at 2:00 a.m. so they went to their respective rooms. Nate made a lunch date with Nadia for the next day.

Everyone in the group went scuba diving the next morning, before Nate and Nadia went to lunch. Nadia couldn't believe how beautiful the coral reefs were and how much fun it was to explore the ocean world.

On Saturday they all went golfing: Nadia, Nate and Sandy on one team and Sal, Tom, Elaine and Carrie on another. The agreement was that whoever lost the match had to plan the activities for Sunday and pay the bill. Nadia hadn't touched her golf clubs in seven months but she played the game of her life. Nate could hit the ball a country mile but where it would land was questionable, while Nadia's drives were long, clean and right down the fairway.

It seemed as if her partners couldn't ask enough questions: "Have you played this game forever? Do you have a PGA rated course in your hometown? Are you going to play for the University?" Nadia just smiled. She was used to hearing questions and comments about her golf performance from the men golfers in her hometown.

Nadia's team won all 18 holes. Sandy was absolutely giddy—never in all her years of marriage to Sal had she ever beaten him in golf. They enjoyed dinner at the clubhouse, after which they arranged tee times for tomorrow. The teams would change, however; Sal and Tom wanted to play with Nadia.

As they were walking to the cars, Nate asked Nadia, "Hey, Farm Girl, where did that talent come from?"

"I don't know, but it used to drive the men in the clubhouse crazy when I'd come in and tell them what I'd shot. They used to accuse me of cheating! Kevin would set them straight and would challenge them to play me. I never did get many offers. I don't think many men would take the chance of getting beaten by a girl."

Carrie joined them on the ride back to the motel. When she suggested to Nadia that they go out that night, Nate asked if he could join them. Nadia couldn't help but needle him a little. "You'd better stay home and rest up for tomorrow. You're going to need all the help you can get to beat me."

Carrie shrugged her shoulders. "The night will consist of a lot of girl talk. If you're up to that, come along." Nate stayed home.

It became clear to Nadia that Carrie had a hidden agenda for their night out when she started talking. "You know that Nate is madly in love with you, Nadia. He told our parents that he didn't care if it took him ten years to convince you to marry him, he'd wait. When we asked him what made you so special, his answer was always the same: 'Just wait until you meet her. You'll fall in love with her too.' You should give Nate a chance, Nadia. He's a good guy—down to earth, honest and faithful. I know how you feel about his looks and how the women throw themselves at him, but he really doesn't care about that. There are more guy athletes who are true to their wives and girlfriends than there are those who fool around. I don't want to lose you as a friend, so forgive me for being pushy, but I also wanted you to know how I feel about my brother."

Nadia thought for a moment before she responded. "Carrie, if I had to write a paper about what I considered to be the perfect man, my paper would be about Nate. I know he's good. I also know that he makes me feel good about myself. It's just that I have so many things I want to pursue before I settle down. I definitely want to get my doctorate in Psychology, and I want to travel to countries where I can work and feel as if I'm making a difference. I wish that I could meet Nate five years from now. I realize that I'm taking a risk by turning him down now, but I truly believe that if he and I are meant to be together, it will happen. Now, let's stop talking about Nate and have a good time. It will probably be five years before I'll be able to do this again!"

Sunday was as wonderful as the previous five days had been. Nadia's golf game was exceptional. Sal and Tom had arranged to have both of the golf pros from the club follow them. Nadia had no idea this was happening, and she was content to just have a good time. On the fifth hole, Sal asked the two men playing behind them if they'd like to play through.

"No, we're enjoying ourselves. It's exciting to watch this young girl hit the ball."

If the other people in her group thought that Nadia played well yesterday, they were in for a real treat today. Nadia's shots were the best ever—crisp and on target. She was having a little difficulty putting, but no one seemed to care. She was in the company of two older men who were doing everything in their power to beat her. So far it wasn't happening.

All of them stopped for a quick snack and drink at the end of nine holes. To their surprise the two gentlemen didn't putt out on nine; instead, they joined the group. Nadia fielded their questions: "Have you played golf all your life? Do you prefer Top Flite or Pinnacles? Have you ever tried using the 'Big Daddy'?"

"No, no, and no," Nadia said. "I golfed at home with my older brother but we didn't have much time. I lived on a farm and there was always so much work to do."

The men were impressed. "Nadia, you're a natural."

"Well, that may be, but right now I have to win a bet with my boyfriend."

Nate overheard and walked over to her. "Did I hear correctly? Boyfriend? You can bet that I'm holding on to that term."

Nadia wanted to grab him right then and there and tell him how she really felt about him—how the thought of him being in Florida for a month while she was in Minneapolis was killing her. When she became aware of her thoughts, the realization hit that he was, indeed, her boyfriend and she didn't want to lose him.

"Okay, let's get this show on the road." Everyone turned to their golf game once again. Nadia was up first. She had a horrible 12th hole; it was a par three and she got a five. Nate finished with a four. He couldn't contain his excitement. "I won! And, as my prize for winning, I'd like to meet your parents." And that was how his first trip to the farm became a reality.

Nate and Nadia spent that evening together. They ate dinner at the Crab Shack, tossing aside all attempts to be neat. Afterward they took a long walk on the beach before returning to the hotel, where it was quiet because most of the guests had already left.

Nate kissed Nadia and told her that he loved her. She told him that she felt the same way. "I have loved you from the very first time we met."

Carrie was watching television when Nadia entered the room. She came to attention when Nadia said, "I told Nate that I loved him."

Carrie's exclamation was loud enough to get Nate's attention in the next room, and he knocked on their door to find out if everything was all right. Carrie let him in and gave him a hug. "I'm so happy I could scream," she said.

"You just did! Let's watch a movie."

The atmosphere on the flight back to Miami was somber. Maybe everyone felt the way Nadia did. She wondered if she would ever be able to duplicate such a wonderful vacation.

Everyone went his separate way in Miami. Sal and Sandy drove to their home; Tom and Elaine flew to Sioux Falls; Carrie went back to Boston College; Nate hailed a cab to take him to spring training; and Nadia flew back to Minneapolis. Promises to stay in touch were shared by all.

Nadia listened as the pilot told them what to expect upon touchdown in Minneapolis: three inches of snow and more falling. He speculated that the runways would be closed shortly. "Welcome back to the real world," Nadia told herself.

Nadia was relieved when she walked into the dorm to find that everything seemed to be the same as when she left. She sat in the lobby for a while, watching the snow-clad students drift in.

As soon as she got to her room, she picked up the phone to talk with her parents. She had missed them while in the Bahamas, so much so that she had called them three times during the week. It made her feel sad—and a little guilty—to be reminded of how hard they worked and still had no money for vacations. She vowed that as soon as she started making money she would take them both on the vacation of a lifetime.

Mary answered the phone. She could barely get a word in while Nadia described her vacation, but was at full attention when she heard the words, ". . . . and he'll be joining us for Easter." The quiet that followed was unnerving.

"Nadia, what are we going to do? How will we entertain someone like Nate? What if he doesn't enjoy himself?" Nadia heard the concern in Mary's voice.

"Well, Mom, we are going to do everything just like we're used to doing it. If he isn't happy being with my family, then I'd better find that out now. I think you'll be pleasantly surprised when you meet him though. I've already called Kevin and Ginny."

The conversation ended with talk about the weather. Mary said that schools had already been closed because of the eight inches of snow on the ground and more on the way. Nadia went to bed, wondering what the new semester held for her.

She awoke with a start and realized instantly that she had missed her first class of the new semester—a great start! Then she became aware of the absence of hallway noise, which usually woke her up. A glance out the window told the whole story. There was so much snow on the ground that it was impossible to tell where anything was in the courtyard, and it was still coming down in sheets. She turned on the TV to confirm what she already suspected: classes at the University had been cancelled. Instead of going back to bed, she settled down to catch up on some reading for one of her year-long courses.

Just as she got comfortable, Nate called to tell her they were on their way to play the White Sox. He asked Nadia how she was feeling.

"Tired. I fell asleep right after I talked to Mom and Dad last night."

"I wish you were here. I miss you. Be safe and stay warm." Nadia felt comforted by his words. It really was a great feeling to be in love!

The University opened the next day, and classes were held for those who were able to attend. The snow was still a major factor in getting to and from classes. But the sun was shining and the temperatures were climbing. Nadia felt good.

Nate kept her informed about spring training; he was increasingly enthusiastic about the up and coming season. He said that all of the players from last year were back and the Twins should be competitive for the title. The news that he would be in Minneapolis on Good Friday to pick her up for the trip home buoyed Nadia's spirits, so that she could hardly concentrate.

A call from her father later in the day, however, put Nate's introduction to the family in perspective. "Your mother is cleaning in places I never knew existed in the house. I made her quit when she wanted to scrub the shelves in the garage!"

"Tell her to relax, Dad. Really, Nate is no different from the rest of us."

"Easier said than done. But I'll do my best. We're looking forward to having you home."

Nadia worked all weekend and into the next week on a paper that had to be completed before she left on Friday. Since the weather was pretty dreadful—cold and wind—she didn't mind spending most of her free moments in the library.

Sal called to find out how she survived the Minneapolis storm and to tell her how much he and Sandy had enjoyed their week with everyone.

Nadia found it easy to talk to Sal. She thanked him again for the wonderful time. When he didn't end the conversation, she knew he had another reason for calling. She was right.

"Nadia, I received another call from the golf pros. They want you to try out for the LPGA. They will work with you this summer and go with you to Phoenix in September for tryouts. They are a hundred percent convinced that you would make the cut. I don't want your answer now because I think I know what it would be. Take your time. Weigh the pros and cons and call me later. I'll try to answer any questions you have. I also have a phone number for one of the pros. You can call him if you'd like. I don't want you to quit college, but you can think about transferring to Arizona State."

"Sal, I don't want to go. It's too far from home. I'd never get to see my parents."

"This is why I don't want an answer right now. Talk it over with your family and Nate. I want you to know that Sandy and I would pay all expenses."

This was just one more tough decision that Nadia needed to make. Was it her imagination or was life getting more complicated? Everything was going too fast, and she was overwhelmed. She resisted the urge to just go to sleep and not think about anything.

Nate and the Twins flew in on Thursday night. The regular season would begin the day after Easter. They decided they would have to drive to the farm that night so they'd have all day Friday to be with her family. Nate was excited but a bit apprehensive about meeting everyone.

"I hope Kevin will be there. I think he'll be my saving grace."

"Yup, I agree, because Ray will probably give you the once over. I'm not convinced that he's real excited about 'his little girl' dating a baseball player."

"Thanks a lot, Nadia. Like my nerves aren't frayed already."

They took turns driving so neither of them would have to sleep the next day away. They arrived at the farm at 8:00. Ray, Mary, Kevin, Katie, Ginny, and Buford came out to greet them.

"Hey everybody, this is Nate." Nadia proceeded to introduce them individually. Hugs and handshakes followed with Nadia wondering why she had worried so much about him fitting in. Mary took Nate's hand.

"It's so nice to have you here, Nate. Kevin will show you where your bedroom is, then come down and join us for breakfast."

The conversation was easy. It was as though Nate had been a part of this family for much longer than two hours. The four men headed outside. On the way through the kitchen, Nate stopped, gave Nadia a kiss and noticed something rolled up on a plate.

"What's that?"

"Lefse. My Mom makes it for all the holidays."

"Mary, can I try it?"

"Of course!"

Four pieces later he headed out the door. "Now, that lefse, or whatever it's called, is the best food I've ever eaten."

Mary was smiling as she told Nadia that Nate seemed to be a good man. "And I must admit he's extremely good looking, not to mention possessing a huge appetite."

Nadia smiled just as Kevin entered the room and announced, "We're going mud running. Any of you fine young ladies interested?"

"Follow me." Kevin motioned to Nate, "I've got some old jeans and a sweatshirt for you to put on. As great as Mom is at getting out mud stains, those new duds of yours would never be wearable again."

Nadia had to admit that Nate wore the farm clothes well. She heard him ask Mary if he could have one more piece of lefse before they left. He said that he had never eaten anything so good.

Mary, of course, gave him a piece and then put four extra rolled pieces in a bag and handed it to him. "For the road; you might get hungry."

Just as they were leaving the house, the phone rang. Nadia answered. It was Jackie. "Hi, Jackie, oh I wish you were here. We're all going mud running. Tony brought over a couple of machines so we each have one. It's beautiful outside. No, you can't talk to him. He'd absolutely die. You can visit with Mom, though. She'll clue you in."

She handed Mary the phone. "You can fill her in on all the details about Nate." Mud running wasn't one of Mary's favorite pastimes, so she was happy to stay home and talk to Jackie. She also wanted to start cutting and chopping everything for the Oof-dah tacos.

The mud running crew was ready to go. Ray led the way. The trails took them deep into the forest and then disappeared.

The riders found themselves deep in the swamp and bogs where mud, water and grass flew up in force. If one was lucky enough to be in the lead, it wasn't quite so bad. Kevin took no mercy on Nate. At each turn he tried to get in front of him and spin the wheels.

Nate's face and every part of his body were caked in mud. Nadia had tears running down her face from laughing so hard. Shame on Kevin for taking advantage of a city boy! Ray stopped several times to ask of they'd had enough. They yelled in unison, "No!"

Finally Ray declared that he'd had more than he could take. He left them with one order: "Be home no later than 4:00 or you'll be at the receiving end of your mother's wrath."

They went full force until Kevin gave the signal. It turned out that he should never have stopped next to a big puddle of water, because, before he could get his machine running again, Nate pulled ahead and gunned the four-wheeler. Kevin was unrecognizable and Nate was triumphant. "Yes! Now, we can go home!" Everyone laughed and pulled out.

They pulled into the yard at 4:05. All machines and drivers were ordered to the well house to clean up until they were decent enough to enter the house. Mary met them outside, "I'll take all the clothes and wash them. Put them in the wash bin in the laundry."

Nadia overheard Katie ask Nate if he was enjoying himself.

"I never thought I could enjoy being with another family as much as I love being with my own. These people are fantastic."

"Oh, you don't have to tell me. I've been with Kevin for over a year and every time I leave this farm it gets more difficult."

He asked her many questions about Nadia. They had visited, still in their mud clothes, for about forty-five minutes when Kevin came out the door.

"All right you two, you've hashed us over long enough!"

The three of them laughed and continued to visit. The only part of the conversation Nadia heard was "relax, man, she isn't going anywhere."

"You'd best get cleaned up," Kevin said to Nate. "Mom has a real treat for you for supper."

The family gathered at the table. Katie and Ginny wanted to help Mary but she would have nothing to do with the idea. She had fried the bread for the Off-dah tacos earlier and kept it warm in the oven. The feast was on.

Nadia told Nate, "Just do what I do. Put whatever you want on this fried bread and then top it off with sour cream and salsa."

"You got it, Farm Girl."

It was amusing and entertaining to watch him. Everyone, including Kevin and Tony, was full after two tacos, but not Nate. "I think I'll have one more."

"Go for it," Nadia said, "You'll be first person I've ever known to be able to eat three." And he did! Mary offered everyone homemade blueberry pie and ice cream. Nate enthusiastically accepted her offer.

His food intake astounded Nadia. "Where in that body are you putting all this food? You'll have to run back to Minneapolis to get rid of all the calories."

"Ah, Nadia, lighten up. As soon as I get back to cooking for myself or having to eat out all the time, these excess pounds will be gone." With that he polished off his pie and ice cream.

It started raining after dinner. Out came Monopoly. The next five hours were spent wheeling and dealing. Ray didn't have to issue his usual command to go to bed. Nadia, Katie and Ginny, who were all getting massacred, were the first to leave. Mary followed. Kevin, Tony and Nate played far into the night.

On Saturday morning the guys went out and fed the cattle and worked on the tractor. Nadia was a little concerned about

Nate being able to handle these jobs, but he apparently had no difficulty. Mary went out to ask them what they'd like to do for supper, eat out or at home.

Nate didn't hesitate. "Eat at home. You're a great cook, and I've got only one more day to enjoy it."

Mary asked him what he'd like to eat. "Anything. Whatever it is, I'll love it."

With that, the women went into town to do some shopping. It was great seeing and visiting with friends. Nadia loved the owner of the grocery store. A gentleman in his seventies, his wife had passed away nine years ago, so every minute of his life was spent at the store. She told him about her boyfriend and how much he was enjoying Mary's cooking.

"Then, Mary, I believe you should make your famous meatballs and gravy," Mr. Johnson suggested. On the way out of the store, Mary invited him to supper. Mr. Johnson happily accepted the invitation.

Nadia, Ginny, Katie and Mary went to the only women's clothing store in town where Mary insisted on buying each of them a new outfit for Easter Sunday. "Quite a last-minute extravagance," Nadia thought.

Once at home, they boiled three dozen eggs, which they planned to color and decorate after dinner. Despite the fact that they weren't kids anymore, Ray still played Easter Bunny and hid eggs and baskets for everyone. It was obvious to anyone who observed him that he enjoyed being with his kids and their friends who, at this moment, were putting some finishing touches on Mary's sled, including a heater for ultimate comfort.

Mr. Johnson arrived promptly at 6:00, carrying a beautiful bouquet of flowers for Mary. The meatballs deserved their reputation; not a single one was left when everyone finished. Nate even cleaned up the remaining gravy with a slice of bread. Kevin whistled, "And everyone here thinks that I eat a lot! You, my boy, are the champion." Nate took the remark as a compliment and continued to wipe up the faint swipes of gravy remaining on his plate.

It turned out that Mr. Johnson knew more about baseball than anyone: every stat and every story about every team. He told them when he was leaving that it was the best night he'd had in nine years. "See you all in church."

They got everything ready to color the eggs. As Mary was lining up the cups, Nate asked her what she was doing. "We aren't going to eat again, are we?"

"No," Mary replied, "This is another tradition for our family that you probably haven't pursued since you were little. But the Olson family refuses to abandon the Easter Bunny! We even have an egg coloring contest—prizes for the most beautiful and creative egg as well as for the ugliest. So let's see what you can do." She pushed four eggs in front of Nate who, for the next thirty minutes, worked to win a prize.

It so happened that Nate did win a prize—for the most beautiful. He had carefully and painstakingly dipped his egg to make a cross. It took forever, but the final product was worth the wait. Nadia wondered if she was seeing another side of this man she had fallen in love with. Athletic and creative—how much better could it get?

Nate accepted his prize—a ten dollar bill—from Mary and declared that he would never spend it. "It will be a constant reminder of my first trip to the farm."

They played whist and gin rummy far into the night but were still able to respond to Mary's wakeup call the next morning. They all attended the 8 o'clock service, decked out in their finest. It would take a lot more than a night of card playing to keep the Olsons from church on Sunday morning.

Pastor Jim met them at the door and waited until they were seated before introducing Nate to the congregation. He promised that there would be time after the service to ask Nate questions.

Nadia shook her head. It didn't seem fair that Nate would have to be exposed to this kind of scrutiny.

After singing the same wonderful, familiar hymns—"In the Cross," "He Arose," and "He Lives"—Nate graciously fielded all of the questions that were asked from people young and old. Nadia stood by his side, feeling proud of the man who had become her best friend.

The egg hunt began as soon as Nadia and Nate arrived home. Nadia couldn't help but think that if anyone from the outside world had been watching, he would have been amused at the scene: five adults running all over the yard, bending down and cheering at each discovered egg. And every egg had to be found—all 36 of them. When Nate found his basket, he was touched by the contents: homemade jars of jam, jelly, pickles, and salsa as well as boxes of crackers, a bag of Doritos and chocolate chip cookies. Tucked into the basket was an envelope that said, "To be read at a later date." He packed everything back in his basket and brought it to the car. Nadia realized that he had tears in his eyes. When she walked over to him, he said, "I love you, Nadia." He took her hand as they walked into the house.

"I'm sorry. I didn't mean to keep everyone waiting. Thank you, Mary, for my basket of goodies." Nate was very quiet during dinner and consumed half the amount of food as usual. Ray asked what time they would be leaving, and Nate told him they wanted to be on the road as soon as dinner was over.

It took a long time for Nate and Kevin to say their goodbye. Nadia, on the other hand, found it easy to say goodbye, since she would be home for the summer in a few weeks. Nate thanked Ray and Mary and told them he hoped he would be invited to the farm again.

As they pulled onto the highway, Nate stopped the car and asked Nadia to drive. "I just can't do it now, Nadia."

"What's wrong, Nate? Everyone loved you. Why are you so sad?"

"I don't know."

The next eighty miles were wretched; not a word was spoken. Finally, Nadia couldn't stand it any longer. She stopped the car and demanded to know what was going on.

Nate looked at her. "The weekend was great. I enjoyed every minute with your family. They made me feel so welcome, as if I had been with them forever. But when I called home to wish Mom and Dad a Happy Easter, Dad informed me that Sal had called with the news that both of the golf pros were going to be in Minneapolis tomorrow at noon and want to see you."

"So? What's the big deal?"

"Nadia, do you realize the distance there would be between us if you go to Arizona? With my schedule and you in training while going to school—we'd never see each other."

"Oh, for Pete's sake, stop. I am not going and if I did, do you think I'd forget about you? I doubt that would happen. You need to have a little faith in our relationship. I know that I have needed to trust you from the very beginning, and now you need to trust me."

Nate got behind the wheel. "You know, if I could, I think I would retire today and move to the farm. I realize it's not all fun and games like the last few days, but I would buy a few acres and work with Kevin. He's a great guy. The more time I spend with him, the easier it is for me to understand you and your personality."

They stopped at the next gas station to fill up with gas and pick up a couple of Diet Cokes. On the road once more, the conversation continued. "Nadia, do you ever think about us getting married?"

"No, I can honestly say that I haven't. I'm only nineteen and want to finish college and do some things before I settle down."

"Can you imagine yourself being with someone other than me?"

"Absolutely not. I've got it made with you! I can't think of anyone I know who has a life as easy as the one I have—paid for college education, car, vacation in faraway places, money in the bank—I'd have to be crazy to let you go!"

"Is that the only reason you're keeping me on—to make life easier for you?"

"Nah, you're also pretty good-looking."

"Okay, okay, now I know you're being a smart ass."

The rest of the drive was spent joshing one another and enjoying each other's company. They both knew that time together was at a premium with Nate's heavy baseball schedule—over a hundred games from April to October.

Nadia was thinking about how Ginny and Kevin would be graduating in May. She couldn't help but wish it were she who was graduating. All she really wanted to do was spend the entire summer at home.

Nate noticed that she was deep in thought. "Earth to Nadia. Where are you at this moment? Mowing the lawn, hauling bales, eating dinner with your family? I can't bear to think about the middle of May, knowing that you'll be four hundred miles from Minneapolis. You'll come and watch a few games here, won't you?"

"Ah, I'll have to check my social calendar for the summer before I make any commitments."

They arrived at her dorm around nine. Nate kissed her several times, and Nadia wanted more. She felt secure and loved when she was in his arms.

"We'll be leaving tomorrow for Tampa Bay and then to Boston. Guess I'll be going through withdrawal immediately, but then we're home for three games against Detroit. Do you have your tickets?"

"Sure do." They pulled apart and said goodbye when Nadia announced that she had to get inside. A friend of Nadia's had been watching them from the window and told Nadia when she opened the door, "I get jealous every time I see the two of you. Someday I'm going to have a boyfriend exactly like Nate."

Time flew by. As it turned out, Nadia could attend only one of Nate's games. She had straight As so far and didn't want to do anything to jeopardize her record, so she ended up studying a lot. On May 17th, she had her last final exam. Feeling positive about how she had done on all of her finals, she ran up to her room, grabbed her one remaining suitcase (she had packed the car the night before), and headed north. It had been a relief to find out that she could have her old room back next year, so she didn't have to do anything about removing furniture. Now she had seven and a half hours to be alone with her thoughts.

Home at last! The thought of three whole months of working side by side with her Dad and Kevin and doing things with her Mom and sisters produced a huge smile on Nadia's face. She wondered if every college student felt the same way about home, to some extent. Mostly she heard her friends talk about the trips they would be taking this summer.

The action at the Olson house began as soon as she was unpacked. They had to leave for Grand Forks the next day for Ginny's graduation, which would be celebrated with dinner at a good restaurant. Ray and Mary had gotten Ginny a cherry red used car, which was in great shape with low mileage. Kevin and Katie thought about some cool car accessories, and Nadia decided Ginny needed a camera.

Graduation was long and boring. It didn't take the Olsons many minutes to clear out of the gymnasium and head to the motel. Ginny was more than ready to be done with college and get on with her life.

They had a fabulous dinner at Red Lobster. Ginny opened her presents and exhibited great delight at each one, especially news of the car that was waiting for her when she arrived home. She loved the beautiful bag Jackie's Filipino grandmother had made for Jackie to give to her sister. After the presents were opened,

Ginny picked up a card from the table. It was from Nate, who had also enclosed a check, the amount of which Ginny didn't disclose, but Nadia noticed her face reddening when she looked at it.

At 8:00, Tony walked in to the restaurant, and Ginny ran to meet him. Tony had grown up with four brothers and two sisters in Detroit Lakes, so he loved being with the Olson family. His youngest brother had Down Syndrome, a fact that had propelled Tony to major in Special Education at UND and teach children with special needs in Grand Forks.

Tony went directly over to Ray. "Ray, I would like your permission to marry Ginny."

Ray didn't blink. He knew that was coming and was prepared with an answer. "I heartily give you my permission to marry my daughter. I don't know you very well, but if Ginny loves you and you love her, you will be a great addition to the family."

With that, Tony asked Ginny to marry him. She said yes, and he placed a beautiful diamond ring on her finger. Nadia thought about how the family was growing and wished that Jackie could be here for this important event. Two years was too long to be absent from your family.

The Olsons went back to the hotel and played cards for a couple of hours until Mary reminded them that they had to be at Kevin and Katie's graduation at 1:00 the next day.

They made it to graduation with five minutes to spare. Katie's parents were pacing when the Olsons drove up and were visibly relieved to see them. Kevin's graduation ceremony seemed to be shorter than Ginny's, so the Olsons had more time to visit with Katie's parents at their home in Karlstad. Not being much of a "partier," Ray was happy when Mary announced that it was probably time for them to head for home.

As they pulled into their driveway, everybody exclaimed at once, "What's that new pickup doing beside Ginny's car?" Kevin grinned, "It's mine from Nate." It was obvious that Ray had been in on the surprise and had taped the card from Nate to the hood of the pickup. Kevin read the card out loud: "Congratulations, Kevin! Enjoy the pickup. I hope I will be seeing all of you guys at a couple of games this summer. Nate."

Kevin and Ginny took their new vehicles for a drive, while Ray checked the cattle and Mary tussled in the kitchen. Before long, everyone was either in bed or making plans to go to bed. Nadia waited until it was quiet and called Nate. Their conversation was suffused with comments about how much they missed each other. They tried to figure out when Nadia would be able to come to Minneapolis and watch a couple of his games.

The next day was marked by typical farm work: working on the yard, planting the garden, disking the fields, checking on the calves that had been born, and generally getting ready for summer. Spring was a wonderfully busy time on the farm.

Nadia, Ginny and Kevin played as much golf as they could, mostly on Sundays when everyone rested. Nadia was happy to note that her game was still intact. Kevin and Ginny couldn't keep up with her. Kevin said, "You have to go to Arizona, Nadia. Go see how you stack up with the others. There's no downside to doing that."

"I just don't want to be that far away from home."

"And you think that's going to be a problem? Don't worry. Nate will make sure that you will be able to fly home as often as you'd like."

"I'll think about it, but I really don't believe I'm good enough."

She enjoyed spending time with Kevin. They really were good friends.

Summer was wonderful. The Olsons worked extremely hard but they were also rewarded with good times. On the third weekend in June, Nadia, Kevin and Ginny picked up Katie and Tony in Grand Forks and headed to Minneapolis. The Twins played on Friday and Saturday nights and on Sunday afternoon.

The plan was to meet Nate at the motel on Friday, a couple of hours before he'd have to leave for the game.

Nate had gotten great tickets for the Olson clan: first row, right in front of where the pitchers and catchers warm up. The Twins were having a fantastic year and right now were forty-nine and ten. It turned out that Tony was a baseball fanatic, and Ginny would have enjoyed any sport as long as she was sitting next to him. After the game, which the Twins won, everyone headed to the Clubhouse to pick up Nate and five other players who wanted to have dinner with them. Nate wasn't completely happy with the additional company but went along with the plans.

They ended up at a bar and grill in the St. Anthony Falls area. The noise level could have broken the sound barrier. Plans for Saturday were discussed in a jubilant atmosphere that can be enjoyed only after a victorious game. Nate lost his patience with the center fielder, who needed to be pulled aside and told that the three girls were all spoken for. Ginny, Katie, and Nadia had a great time: the three of them and eight young, good-looking guys—what could be better than those odds!

Nate was an excellent host for the entire weekend. He made sure they did things that everyone enjoyed. On Monday morning the team flew out at seven, and Nadia found it difficult to say goodbye to Nate. She made up her mind on the way home that she wouldn't go to Arizona—maybe the following year. By that time she would have her BA and it would be easier to transfer. Kevin wasn't very happy with her decision; he thought she was throwing away a chance to make it big in the golf world. They dropped off Tony and then Katie. Ray and Mary were relieved and happy to have everyone home again.

The summer flew by. The Olsons celebrated the 4th of July in their usual manner: food, fun and fireworks. The country fair came and went. There was one real bright spot: Jackie would be home on December 1st. That was four months from today. Mary had a countdown started—120 days. Nadia was extremely excited.

Jackie would be flying into Minneapolis so she would be the first to see her. Anticipation—it definitely made life interesting.

Ginny and Nadia went to the Cities again in August. Nadia wanted to make sure her schedule included all the classes she needed and had signed up for. She knew her schedule would be tough, but it didn't matter because she would have her doctorate at 24.

During the month of August, whenever Mary had extra time, she would sew on Ginny's and Katie's wedding dresses. Both were beautiful and very different from each other. Ginny and Nadia worked hard around the farm to free up Mary for more creative work. Both of the girls had become old hands at canning and freezing vegetables from the garden.

The family members worried about Mary. She never complained but they could tell she wasn't feeling 100 percent. Ray convinced her to make an appointment with the doctor for a complete physical

Then one day Buford went crazy, barking and running back and forth on the deck, whining and pawing the floor. Kevin heard the commotion and stepped outside the shed where he and Ray were working.

"Dad, something's wrong. Buford is trying to tell us something." Ginny and Nadia also heard the noise and met Kevin and Ray at the house. As soon as they opened the door, they saw Mary lying on the kitchen floor, a broken glass next to her. Ginny dialed 911. In less than fifteen minutes the ambulance had arrived and the EMTs were loading Mary on a stretcher. They didn't stop at the small hospital in the neighboring town but kept going to Grand Forks. Kevin was right on the ambulance's tail.

The emergency doctors and nurses were waiting as the ambulance pulled in. After a brief exam, they wheeled Mary into the OR. No one knew exactly what happened but they knew that the situation was serious. They were all thinking the same thing: How could they possibly live without Mary's love and guidance? Nadia's heart went out to Ray. Big tough man that he was, he couldn't hold back the tears. The kids tried to console him but weren't much help, since they were crying even harder.

After what seemed like hours, the doctor came into the waiting room and gave them the news: Mary had suffered a massive heart attack and had undergone open heart surgery. She would be out for several hours. The doctor suggested they all could go up to recovery in an hour but Ray thought it would be best if they went immediately.

Nadia tried calling Jackie and ended up leaving a message at the Peace Corps office in Manila. The staff there said they would do everything possible to contact Jackie and give her the message. Nadia thought several times about calling Nate, but something prevented her from acting on her intentions every time. She just didn't want to leave her family for one minute; they all needed each other. Kevin called Katie who called the pastor and asked him for prayers from the congregation. They kept a close eye on Ray who wasn't doing very well. Three hours after the doctor had talked with them, they were allowed to go in and see Mary. Nadia was horrified; there were tubes coming in and out of her body. Mary recognized them, but that was it. Sleep was what her body needed.

The staff was fantastic. The Olsons had arrived without anything and were given toothbrushes, toothpaste, combs and deodorant without having to ask for them. The next two days were filled with anxiety—marked by ups and downs. On the third day Mary got out of bed. The nurses wanted her to go for a short walk but she got very dizzy and threw up. Nadia had to leave; this was not her mother.

"Please God, take care of Mom. Don't take her from us. We need her so badly." She prayed harder than she had ever prayed in her life.

The next couple of days brought improvements in Mary's condition. Her children and husband relaxed a bit and even got a motel room. They drove to Wal-Mart and picked up some essentials for everyone, including Ray who refused to go with them. On the fourth day, they pried Ray from the room so he could take a shower and sleep for eight uninterrupted hours. Mary was never alone during this entire time, each one taking a turn to sit and mostly just watch her sleep. Pastor Jim came, loaded down with cards and flowers. He also had wonderful news for Ray and Kevin.

"Don't worry about the farm. Your neighbors are taking care of everything—canning, keeping up with the vegetable harvest. Oh, by the way, I've got Buford at our house. You may not get him back."

Mary smiled more during his visit than she had in the last six days. Because she was showing great improvement, her family could anticipate bringing her home. Jackie had been calling on a daily basis. She wanted to come home, but they assured her that it wasn't necessary; everything was going well.

On Saturday afternoon they did some grocery shopping and brought back McDonalds for Ray and everyone else. Then they all joined Mary for dinner. It really was a joyous occasion; one would have thought they were celebrating Thanksgiving.

After the doctor's final rounds that evening, the Olsons were confident that they would be able to take Mary home the next day. But it was not to be. At 2:00 the next morning, Nadia heard the phone ringing and, before she could speak, heard the concern in the nurse's voice.

"Your mother's condition is deteriorating. You'd better come."

Nadia screamed, "Mom's dying."

Nadia and the others were back at the hospital in record time. Mary was in surgery by the time they got there. Her temperature had jumped to 104 degrees. They waited and paced until a nurse finally came out to give them an update.

"Mary has an infection. The doctors are giving her the strongest dose of antibiotics possible through IVs. The next twelve hours will be crucial."

The waiting was unbearable. The whole family sat and paced until Nadia thought she would scream. Finally, the doctor came out to see them.

"Mary's temperature is slowly coming down. Ray, would you like to sit with her? You'll have to put on a gown and mask."

Nadia had to ask, "What about us kids? Can we see her?"

"Sorry, right now we can't take a chance with a lot of people. Try to relax. We will keep you updated."

A call came in for any member of the family. Kevin took it. It was Pastor Jim wondering when the Olsons would be leaving, since the congregation wanted to have dinner ready and waiting for them when they arrived home. Kevin explained what had happened and that, at this time, they didn't know much. He asked Pastor Jim to continue praying for Mary.

Before they ended the conversation, Pastor Jim told Kevin to tell Nadia that Nate had called several times and wanted to speak with her. Nadia received the news but did nothing about calling him.

Jackie called and said that she was flying home immediately. Ray had a hard time but finally convinced her that getting on the next plane was not necessary at this time. When Nadia heard about Jackie, she knew that she had to call Nate. He deserved to know about Mary.

His first words were, "Nadia, what's going on? Why haven't you called me?"

Nadia tried to explain about Mary, but it was difficult to talk between sobs. Nate grew impatient, "Why didn't you call me right away? I would have been there in two hours."

"Nate, I can't talk. Mom is holding her own. Call Kevin if you want to know more. I have to go." Nadia hung up and joined everyone in the waiting room. Just then, the nurse walked in.

"You can relax now. We are definitely seeing improvement. Your mother's temperature continues to go down. She even smiled at your Dad and squeezed his hand. Maybe one of you could try to get your Dad to leave and have a bite to eat. I'm not going to tell you we're out of the woods, but the doctor is encouraged by her improvement."

Kevin went in and got Ray. Nadia called Jackie again and gave her the most recent news. The doctor then came in with an update. "Your mother is going to pull through. She is very strong and a real fighter."

Everyone exclaimed at once, "Thank you, God."

The next seven days were up and down. Friends, relatives, boyfriends, girlfriends—many people who knew Mary came and went. Andy brought them the news they needed to hear at this point: "No need to worry about the farm. It's in good hands."

Ray commented, "The Man Upstairs must have known this was going to happen. That's why we only planted wheat, rye, and oats. If we would have planted corn it would have made this situation more difficult."

Nadia was glad to hear Ray participate in a conversation. He had been unusually quiet since they brought Mary in two weeks ago.

Mary's temperature was down to 99.3 the next morning. The nurses succeeded in getting her up and took her for a short walk. Mary was exhausted but felt satisfied with her small accomplishment.

It was Nadia's turn to stay with Mary. She read to her after dinner and they watched part of a movie before Mary fell asleep. Nadia was just settling in for the night when the phone rang at the nurses' station. It was Nate.

"Nadia, do you have time to talk to me now? I need to know how your Mom is doing."

"She's doing much better. But this is my turn to stay with her and I need to get back to her room."

"Why don't you include me? I would have thought you wanted me to be with you. I love your mother. And I love you."

"I don't know." She hung up the phone and realized how tired she felt. Assuming they would be able to leave the hospital on Monday, she would have only fifteen days until she'd have to leave for college. How could she possibly leave Mary then? She reminded herself that Ginny and Kevin would be around, but they would be working. She finally concluded that she had to take one day at a time.

The following morning Mary's temperature was normal. The nurses gave her a bath and washed her hair. She even got to put on a pair of sweats and a shirt. The kids took her for three short walks during the course of the day. Then the doctor told them that all of Mary's tests came back normal and they would be able to leave the next day, if her condition continued to improve. He cautioned them that the first two weeks at home would be critical and, to insure that everyone understood the recovery routine, they had to watch a movie about caring for a heart patient after surgery.

True to his word, the doctor signed Mary out in the afternoon. At first, every day at home was treated like a holiday. Then things slowly got back to normal. Ginny went back to work; Kevin and Ray resumed full-time care of the farm. The neighbors had done a great job of keeping things going, but there was still a lot of work to do. They all took advantage of Nadia's presence for two weeks before she left for college. Nadia spent a lot of time with Mary—doing little things such as visiting the many people who had helped out in her absence, attending Bible study, checking in at the school, buying material for quilts. Mary loved it all. She knew that she had to take it easy for a while—no lifting and regular walking—but she didn't seem to mind as long as Nadia was there with her.

In spite of her misgivings about leaving Mary, Nadia was excited when she said goodbye and left the farm for Minneapolis. It was a new year, filled with promises of good things to come. And she was ready for whatever lay in her path.

She arrived at the dorm around 7:30, parked the car and unloaded her things. Classes would begin in a couple of days, and she wanted to be settled in. She tried calling Nate but there was no answer. That had been the case with several phone calls she had made during the past week. He must be pretty busy. She decided that she would go to the game tomorrow and hoped that they would be able to visit.

Nadia was surprised that Sal and Sandy weren't at the game. She had kept in contact with them and they hadn't said anything about being gone.

The players were already on the field ready to play when she arrived. Nadia waited for Nate to acknowledge her, but there was no indication that he was aware of her presence. She waited a few minutes after the game, but it eventually became obvious that he didn't want to see her. Then, just as she was about to leave, Nate emerged from the dugout and walked to where a beautiful girl was waiting. He put his arm around her and they walked out of the stadium together.

Nadia was unprepared for that turn of events. She knew that she had ignored Nate during the time her mother was sick, but it hadn't occurred to her that he would forget about her so soon. She found herself unable to move and stood by the bus stop until they got into his pickup and drove off. She knew that Nate saw her—how could he not have seen her? Ben, another player from the team, approached her and asked if she wanted a ride home.

"Thanks, Ben, but I think a good walk is what I need." Nadia wanted to keep her thoughts to herself, at least until she was able to sort them out.

She was in shock—no denying that! Somehow she found herself back at her room in the dorm where she picked up the phone to call home. Ginny had the day off so she and Mary were having a good time doing things around town. Nadia wanted to talk to them all night, so her mind wouldn't be on Nate. But she fell asleep with the phone in her hand and didn't wake up until the next morning. When she remembered what had happened, she wished that she had stayed asleep.

The next day, Nadia bought her own ticket for the game. She didn't want to use her season ticket, so she had to settle for the nose-bleed section. The Twins had no trouble beating the Orioles. After all, this was their year; they had hung on to the number one spot all season. They were headed for the World Series all right—and they would win. Nadia loved the Twins.

She decided to walk home after the game. Three blocks from campus, a pickup pulled up next to her. She didn't have to look. She knew it was Nate.

"Do you want to talk?"

"No, I'm going to take advantage of the beautiful day; there aren't many days like this left. Have a good evening, Nate." She kept walking and never turned around.

Her phone was ringing when she opened the door. It was Carrie, Nate's sister, calling to ostensibly find out how Mary was, but Nadia knew that she really wanted to know what was going on between her and Nate. Nadia kept the conversation going by asking Carrie questions about her family. Thankfully, they had to say goodbye when there was a knock on Carrie's door. Carrie told Nadia that she would call her back in a couple of days. Nadia hoped that wouldn't happen. She didn't want to be in a position again where she would have to explain things between her and Nate.

Nadia knew that telling her family about Nate would be difficult. She also knew that they'd probably side with Nate. Kevin had begged her daily to call Nate but, for some reason, she either didn't try hard enough to reach him or he didn't want to be reached. She decided that she'd tell her family during MEA.

School kept Nadia busy. It was a relief to be busy. One of her classes was held in a lab with a professor whom Nadia adored. She also had a wonderful lab partner, a young man who took school as seriously as she did. The Psychology Lab was by far her favorite class so far.

Nadia had a paper due at the end of the semester that would count for half her grade. She chose to write on the effects of divorce on children. She was surprised to learn from her research that divorce was becoming so common that a survey conducted in elementary schools in Minnesota showed that 55 % of the students had a different last name than that of their parents. Nadia knew that she and her siblings were among the minority in having both parents at home when the school bus would drop them off. In thinking back, she realized that rarely was there a time when both of her parents hadn't come upstairs to kiss her and her siblings goodnight, and tell them how much they were loved. How blessed they were. She could hardly wait to start writing her paper.

The Twins were out of town for nine days. The last three games of the season would be at home. If they won all five games they would be division champions. The only condition under which Nadia would miss a game was if something happened to Mary and she had to go home. When she inquired about the cost of the series tickets, she wished that she were either rich or Nate's girlfriend again, but she bought a ticket anyway.

Every time Nadia called home, the news about Mary got better. Mary had only one more week before she could return to school. Ray was happy to hear that news. "Let me tell you, it can't come fast enough. She's driving us all crazy!"

Sal called one evening. He and Sandy had been out east visiting their family and getting their son settled in college for another year. Nadia was happy to hear from him. "It's been ages since I talked to you. How is everything?"

"We're great, but we've missed you. How's your mother . . . . and the farm?" Minutes of casual conversation and then came the question that Nadia expected: "What happened between you and Nate, Nadia?"

"I honestly don't know. You'll have to ask him."

"And I will. In the meantime, how would you like tickets for all of the playoff games?"

Nadia could hardly contain her excitement and appreciation. "Thank you. Thank you so much. You must know how much that means to me."

No sooner had she hung up the phone when it ran again. It was Nate.

"Nadia, I have to talk to you."

"Too bad, drop dead. Talk to your girlfriend."

Nadia had to listen to the phone ring several times. She didn't want to turn it off in case someone from home called.

Concentrating so hard on her paper, Nadia didn't hear the knock on her door. Elaine stuck her head in the door. "Nadia, could you come downstairs for a second?

She saw Nate standing next to Elaine and almost did an about face, but he grabbed her arm. "Please, give me just a minute."

"You have exactly sixty seconds, so you'd better start talking."

"What I need to know is why you didn't call me when your mother was in the hospital." Nate looked the part of a concerned friend, but Nadia didn't buy it.

"Are you crazy? My mother was dying and I was supposed to call you? Actually, I did try to call you but never got an answer. Anyway, my only concern at that time was having Mom get well. Regardless, what you did to me to get even was immature and inexcusable. I'm going on with my life without you. It's over, Nate. Now, if you'll excuse me, I've got a lot of work to do. Have a good life."

It felt good to get that off her chest. During the whole time she and Nate had dated, Nadia was in love with him but never felt totally comfortable: there were just too many differences. Maybe if they had met a few years later, the divide wouldn't have been so great.

The days flew by. Life was good. Mary was healthy and enjoyed going to school every day. The Twins would be starting the playoffs shortly. Best of all, Nadia loved how the semester was going. Toby, her lab partner, had become a good friend; they worked together, ran together and spent hours in the library together. He invited her to spend the weekend at his home in Stillwater.

What an experience that was! Toby's three brothers and a sister had already graduated from college and moved out, so they weren't around. His parents couldn't handle the empty nest syndrome, so they had adopted four young children—age two to seven. And they were definitely around! Nadia was used to activity and commotion in a home, but this was unreal! After spending two days with Toby's family, she could understand why he always told her he had to come back to school to rest.

After learning about the children's past, Nadia asked Toby's parents if she could use them as part of her research paper. They would, of course, remain anonymous. They both agreed and were eager to give Nadia more information. She learned that the four children had lived in a home with an alcoholic mother and her numerous boyfriends. Their father had split after the fourth child was born. The only time the oldest boy could ever remember either his mother or father being nice was in the morning. He told his new parents that by the time the big hand and the little hand on the clock were on twelve, his parents were fighting and hitting each other. The children would be locked in a closet every day that they fought.

The seven-year-old entered the room at that time. He told Nadia, "We'd have to stay in the closet all day. We would pee and poop in a corner and at night I had to clean it up. If my baby sister pooped in her pants, I would get hit with the belt ten times. We got to eat once a day. One time we got so hungry that we started beating on the door. We never did that again because my father beat us so bad we were bleeding. Just before we escaped, I never ate any of my food. I would chew it up really good and then put it in my baby sister's mouth."

Nadia was horrified. She wanted him to stop, but the stories poured out of his little mouth—some so horrible that Nadia knew she couldn't publish them in her paper. Toby's mother picked up where the little boy left off. "When the children were found on the side of the road, they were a sight to behold. The sheriff told the court that he had never seen anything close to it before. There was so much feces on their bodies, it was difficult to tell what nationality they were."

She continued, "The night before they escaped, the mother opened the closet door and smeared her own feces all over their bodies, laughed and closed the door. In her drunken stupor she forgot to lock the door. After it had been quiet for a long time, the little boy lifted his baby sister into his arms and, as quietly as four children could be, he led them out of the house. An elderly man picked them up and brought them directly to the police station. The little boy weighed forty-eight pounds. How he was able to carry his baby sister for many miles is still a mystery. The doctor who attended to the children told the court that if the children had been left in these conditions ten more days, none of them would be around today."

Toby's parents first read this horror story in their local paper. It took two days for them to contact Social Services and tell them they wanted to adopt all four children. They showed Nadia before and after pictures and talked about how they enjoyed watching the children just be children, something they knew the children had been denied all of their lives.

Nadia fell asleep that night thinking about all the children who were suffering through horrors like this. She was determined to make a difference. The weekend convinced her even more that she had chosen the right profession. She wondered if she should look into getting a degree in social work as well as psychology.

Part 4

Sal and Sandy picked Nadia up for the first playoff game. The dome was filled to capacity and the noise was deafening. Nate acknowledged the three of them. Nadia wished, at that moment, that he weren't so good-looking. She wondered if he had the same girlfriend, a new girlfriend, or no girlfriend. Secretly she missed him.

The Twins won the game 7-6. The announcer wished everyone a good night and hoped they would return for the next game. Nadia asked Sal if they'd be going.

"You bet—wouldn't miss it for anything. It's been too many years since we had a team like this."

Nate made his way to their seats. Sal greeted him. "Great game, Boy. It was a joy to watch. Too bad you and Nadia have to fight all of the time. It would have been fun for the four of us to go for a bite to eat. I think both of you should get your act together. Life is too short. Stop being so bull-headed, both of you, and talk it out."

Nadia said, "I don't think that will be happening, but thanks for trying, Sal. There's Nate's new girlfriend over there, waiting for him."

She noticed that the girl waiting for Nate was not the same one she had seen with him before. Not wanting to dwell on the situation she told Sal that she had to go, because she had a meeting with two people from a children's advocacy agency. As it turned out, she made it to her meeting with a couple of minutes to spare.

Growing up in a small community, Nadia felt that she had been shielded from many of the evils in the world. She had never heard of a child being mistreated in the horrible way that the children adopted by Toby's family were. What kind of a parent could or would hurt his own child? She wondered if she would be able to handle situations such as these.

Nadia didn't go to the next game. She was working on her paper and the time got away from her. Feeling guilty for not being there, she was glad to hear that the Twins won so they would play the winner of the White Sox and Cardinal series, which turned out to be the White Sox.

At the first game, fans filled the stadium to capacity. The excitement was palpable—almost too much to bear. The White Sox were up first. Then the unimaginable happened: by the time the top of the inning was over, the score was 9-0. The Twins tried three pitchers but were unable to recover; the nine runs were the only runs the Sox got, but the Twins scored only four times. The season came to an abrupt end. The players and the fans were in shock. Nate looked up for a second and then disappeared. Sal, Sandy, and Nadia just sat there.

Sal spoke first. "What the hell was that? I thought this would be their year. Never mind the fact that the Sox were barely in the running."

Nadia got in the car, but before she could get the door shut, Nate was standing there. "I've gone through every play in the first inning. We didn't make any errors. I thought Beachum pitched fairly well. What happened, Nadia?"

Nadia felt sorry for him. "I wish I could answer that for you. There's always next year or the year after. I don't know. I guess you'll have a bit more time during the off season now. I just hope the owners don't make too many quick judgments about letting players go. You guys need to have one more try at it next year."

"What are your plans?" Nate wanted to know. "Let's go for a pizza—just as friends."

Nadia had missed talking with Nate, and she was hungry, so she agreed. As soon as they sat down, Nate asked, "So what are you doing these days?"

"Same thing every day, I guess: attend class, study for tests and go to bed. I'm going home next week. We have Thursday and Friday off. I can help Mom a little. This is turning out to be such a busy year for our family. I graduate, both Ginny and Kevin are getting married and Jackie comes home. I often wonder how we'll be able to fit it all in and still get the farm work done and build Kevin and Katie's house."

Nate looked straight at her. "Nadia, let me come home with you next weekend. I'd really enjoy visiting with your parents and hanging out with Kevin."

"Nate, no, let's just be friends. I don't believe either of us has room in our lives for more turmoil or anxiety."

"Let me go with you—as your friend."

"No, the whole rigamarole will begin all over. Live your life, Nate. You'll find someone who'll fit your lifestyle and make you happy. I'm thinking about transferring to Arizona to at least give golf a try. I know it's a long shot, but if I don't try, I'll regret it down the road."

"Do Sal and your Dad know?"

"No, and I'd appreciate it if you wouldn't say anything." Nate nodded. And then he left.

Nadia made an appointment with her advisor to talk about transferring for her Masters. Mr. Jackson wasn't happy at the possibility and he said so, "I'd like to have you stay here. We have an excellent golf program. Why don't you go out for it this spring?" He paused, then continued: "However, I can understand why Arizona is the place you want to go. Golf for that state is like hockey to Minnesota."

Nadia gathered her books. "I don't want you to think this is a done deal. It's just something I've been thinking about and I wanted your opinion."

"Nadia, if you have a natural talent, you should make use of it." Mr. Jackson shook her hand. "Go, Nadia, give it your best shot."

The thought of being so far away from her family gave Nadia goose bumps. Mary was healthy and was able to keep up with her daily chores, but she got tired quickly. Ginny was a life saver, but she'd be a married lady in June and who knows where she will end up living. Tony had submitted applications at all of the neighboring school districts. The response was the same everywhere: no Special Ed positions were available right now. Kevin and Katie would be close by, but they both had jobs. Jackie would also be back on home turf, but everyone knew that she wouldn't be around for long; she would be off to save the world again in a matter of a few months. Nadia became tired just thinking about the situation. One good thing was that her decision was still months away. She promised herself that she would do well in school and just enjoy each day.

On Wednesday afternoon she finished her exam and was on the road by 3:00. Life was certainly easier when you had your own vehicle. Plans had been made for the long weekend. Along with doing everything possible with the family, she, Ali and Andy had persuaded many of their classmates to set aside a few hours on Friday night for a get together. Nadia thought about how much fun it will be to see how everyone is doing and how life is treating her friends.

She pulled into the Olson driveway where her mother was standing. "Hi Mom, get over here. I need a hug!"

It was difficult to let go. Good thing Dad and Kevin came out of the shed. Ginny and Tony pulled into the driveway minutes later. Katie would arrive later.

The four days flew by. They were all reminded of Grandma's saying: "The older you get, the faster time goes!" They managed to squeeze in all the things they wanted to do but agreed they'd have to go back to school and work to catch up on sleep!

Ali and Andy were both engaged. They had met their significant others at college. Wedding bells wouldn't ring for another year, since they both wanted to graduate and find employment before they got married. Nadia's friends were shocked to find out that she and Nate weren't seeing each other. "You're crazy" was the phrase most often directed at her.

The Olsons went to church and from there to the best country restaurant in the world for dinner. With a full stomach and many tearful goodbyes, Nadia headed down the road. Her only comfort was that in five weeks, they would all be celebrating Thanksgiving together.

Nadia's drive back to Minneapolis was uneventful as were the next five weeks. The weather was chilly, but there was no snow, so she could run outside and didn't have to resort to the indoor track. She spent one Saturday at Toby's parents' home. There was enough snow at that time to slide down the hill in their backyard. She and Toby left after dinner because Toby had to sing in the choir at the campus early church service. Their relationship reminded Nadia of all the time she and Andy had spent together: no pressure, no pretending—just a strong, close friendship. The admiration she had for Toby's parents grew with each visit.

She called Nate's family on Tuesday evening. Carrie answered. Their conversation was lively, informational and fun. Carrie had been dating a "dude" for a year; he was the son of a huge cattle farmer in Colorado. There was lots of teasing and bantering back and forth.

"Just think, Carrie, you could raise little farm girls."

"If I do, I hope they're just like you. By the way, Nate met a girl in Florida, and I think he's going back down there after Thanksgiving."

"Good. He's a super guy and deserves to be happy."

Nadia headed home for Thanksgiving and enjoyed another fabulous four days of eating and Christmas shopping in Grand Forks on Black Friday. Ginny and Katie tried to convince the men to say home, but to no avail. They hated shopping but loved the idea of being together. This year the Olsons didn't have to spend time looking for items for Jackie. She would be home in a six weeks. Everyone knew that once Jackie was on U.S. soil, Mary would perk right up. Sunday was cookie-baking day, followed by church, and then Nadia was headed home—actually, back to school. She had been at the University so long it certainly seemed like home.

As she drove, her mind wandered to future plans. She would call the University of Arizona and set up a time to visit the campus and, hopefully, get together with the golf coach. Planning her life made the trip go quickly.

Nadia enjoyed an early Christmas with Toby and his family. What a joy each of those visits brought her! Toby's family had already been instrumental in planning her future.

"Someday, Toby, I'll make a difference in many children's lives just as your parents have."

Christmas with Sal and Sandy was fabulous. They had their entire family home for the holidays. Sal was ecstatic. "Two weeks. We get them for two weeks."

Sandy had a schedule set in stone. Nadia was impressed. "How are you ever going to have time to do everything?"

Sandy smiled, "Where there's a will, there's a way. Now, this will be our ocean dinner. Then we'll have a mountain dinner, followed by a prairie dinner, a Bayou dinner and, finally, a Scandinavian dinner," she explained.

As soon as she walked into the house, Nadia was struck by the fact that never in her lifetime had she seen so many gifts. Her first thought was, "What a sin with so many people in the world not even getting one gift." For a brief moment, she found herself disliking this family, and then decided that there must be some explanation.

"Hi, you must be Nadia." She was taken off guard and then looked up to see a gorgeous man. Nate ran through her mind but, of course, he wasn't present.

"Yes, and you must be the famous grandson."

"Yeah, I guess. I'm Seth. It scares the shit out of me to meet new friends of my grandparents. I never know what they've said about me. I saw you staring at the gifts. Only two are for us and the rest, well, that's why you're here so early. We all go to a downtown shelter, serve a meal my Grandma has prepared, and then deliver gifts to everyone there."

"Thank goodness, because to be honest with you, I resented your family there for a minute."

"Nah, when Shelly and I graduated from high school, Sal and Sandy gave us a gift—college paid for and a fair amount of money, under the condition that we kept our grades up. We could do what we wanted to do with our money, but, from that point on, we were on our own. They said that if we spent it wisely it would last a lifetime. And that's the story. Now, they are going to spend every penny they still have. Grandpa and Grandma support more charities than I could ever count. One last thing before we go into the kitchen. I was told that you were "hands off," that you belonged to Nate. Grandpa said that once I saw you and visited with you I'd know what he was talking about. He was right once again."

Nadia giggled. "I'm going to take that as a compliment, but this thing with Nate is over. He has a new girlfriend in Florida, and Carrie told me that he was going back down there to visit her and that she probably would be at their house for Christmas."

With that they joined the rest of the family. They packed up vans, pickups and cars and headed downtown, where they served over two hundred people who enjoyed a turkey dinner with all the trimmings. Then they handed out over five hundred gifts: dolls, wagons, strollers, trucks, coats, boots, mittens, hats and candy. The expressions on the children's faces would remain etched in Nadia's mind forever.

Nadia said, "Thank you, Sal and Sandy, for sharing your wealth." She decided that being rich wasn't all that bad when you shared it with the less fortunate. They all returned to the house, feeling pretty hungry. Excitement overcame them when Sal placed the lobster into the boiling water. Nadia couldn't remember a time when she had been this hungry. The dinner was delicious, although they all agreed with Seth who remarked, "You could have served porridge, Grandma, and we would have eaten it." They exchanged gifts after the kitchen had been cleaned up. Nadia was amazed that Sandy didn't have a maid.

Nadia received a purse from Shelly, Seth's sister, a gold tennis bracelet from their parents, and an outfit from Sal and Sandy. Then she noticed a long white envelope on the bottom of the box. She cried as she read it, "We consider you one of our grandchildren; therefore, we want to do the same for you as we did for them. The money is yours for you to do as you please. Invest it wisely and you won't have to worry financially for the rest of your life." Nadia had never seen a check with so many zeros.

"I just can't accept this."

Sal was nonplussed. "Well, you'll notice that it is a duplicate of the one that has already been deposited into your account."

"But, Sal, I don't need this."

"Honey, this is your future. The road through life has many bumps in it; this gift will make the road less bumpy. No more is to be said. Merry Christmas and Happy New Year."

Nadia handed each of them a gift. Monetarily they weren't worth very much, but she hoped they would realize how much time and love had been spent on choosing them. She didn't have to wait long. Sal and Sandy opened their present. Inside was the most beautiful handmade quilt from Mary, made especially for them, with the red, white and blue colors that represented the Twins. Minutes passed before a word was spoken. Oh, how Nadia wished her Mom could have been a mouse in the corner to see their faces. They unfolded the quilt and realized it was a baseball diamond. Unbelievable! Even Nadia's breath was taken away. How could her mother create such a beautiful quilt with no pattern, just her eyes and hands!

Sandy spoke first, "Nadia, what is your parents' phone number. We'll call your mother right now."

Everything was put on hold until the call ended. Nadia looked at Shelly and Seth to see their reactions. They were waiting patiently while their parents just kept murmuring about the beauty of the quilt. Finally Shelly opened her gift. She loved the hooded sweatshirt from Lake of the Woods. Seth opened his gift, and it was obvious that he liked his Arctic Cat sweatshirt.

"Maybe someday I'll be invited to ride one of these things up North."

Nadia smiled, "Anytime you want to, you're more than welcome."

His comment generated a raised eyebrow from Sal. Seth recognized the gesture as being one of concern for the warning that his grandfather had given him earlier about Nadia belonging to Nate. "Relax, Grandpa, I haven't forgotten." Sal smiled and nodded.

The rest of the evening was spent playing Rummikub, Nadia's gift to the family. When it was time to leave, she felt a pang of sadness. She had grown to love Sal and Sandy and thought of them as grandparents. She most likely wouldn't see them until April when they returned from Florida. Nadia expressed her gratitude for the wonderful evening and, after wishing everyone a Merry

Christmas, she walked out the door. Seth walked her to her car and asked for her phone number. "Just in case," he grinned.

She left for home the following morning. A beautiful sight greeted her when she drove into the yard. White lights adorned the house, barn and garage. Multi-colored lights lit up trees throughout the yard. Jackie immediately came to her mind. This would be the second Christmas she would have to spend away from home, and Nadia wished that Jackie was going to be here this year. She sat in the car and took it all in. Ray and Kevin had worked so hard. Every year they added some new magic. Her favorite would always be Gabriel, a huge angel lit up with white lights. It was her sign that Jesus had sent an angel to watch over them.

Mary appeared in the doorway. "Are you coming in or are you going to spend the night in your car?"

"Oh, Mom, it's so beautiful!"

"Did you notice Rudolph pulling the sleigh on top of the house?"

"Of course, how could I miss him?"

Ray and Kevin joined in welcoming her home. For a while everyone was talking at once. Buford continued to wag his tail, waiting to be loved up.

Kevin, Ray and Nadia walked over to Kevin's lot to see the progress on his house. Nadia couldn't believe that it was almost finished.

"Unreal. I didn't think you were going to start until spring."

"Yeah, but everything went so well this fall, we had time on our hands and the cement pourers were available to do the basement, so we just kept it going from there. We kept the hired hand on when we realized he was a carpenter by trade. This winter Dad and I will continue working on the interior. Well, we'd better get back to the house. Mom has mashed potatoes, meatballs and gravy ready for dinner."

"Oh, I love that lady! I've been dreaming about this meal since I was here at Thanksgiving. Buford, if I eat like this for the next three weeks, you and I will be burning the pavement."

Ray grinned. "By the looks of it, you don't have to worry about putting on a few pounds."

"Oh, Daddy, you are too kind!"

Her bed felt so good that Nadia didn't get up until 9:00. The rest of the day was spent decorating the trees upstairs and downstairs. Mary wrapped gifts while Ginny made fudge and caramels. Kevin was in and out tasting and testing.

After dinner Mary wanted to call Jackie. Ginny was adamant that they should wait until Christmas day. She won the argument, but it took a lot of convincing before Mary would relent.

Kate got home the next day. She had worked every weekend after Thanksgiving until now so she could have eight days off. She would spend Christmas Eve with the Olsons and then she and Kevin would go to her house on Christmas Day. Tony would also be with them for the entire Holiday season. His family had celebrated last weekend because they were going to Haiti for two weeks with their church group. Ginny went to work at 11:00 just as the rest of the family was going to bed. She didn't complain because she had the week off between Christmas and New Years.

Christmas Eve morning was perfect. Big flakes of snow were falling to the ground. The whole family was just sitting down for breakfast when Ginny drove in. Mary looked out the window and was quick to announce that there was another person in the car. Ginny must have met Tony in town. No, that didn't make sense. Who was it then? When she recognized the second person, Mary let out a piercing scream.

"It's Jackie, it's Jackie, it's Jackie!" Those were the only words she could get out.

It turned out that Jackie had called Ginny at work in early November to see if she could keep a secret. When Ginny assured her that she could, Jackie told her that she would be flying in to Grand Forks on December 24th at 5:30 a.m.

Ginny was relieved that she was able to keep the secret. "Can you imagine how many times I just about spilled the beans?"

Tears of joy ran down faces. Kate had been in the shower when all the hoopla was taking place. The look on her face when she entered the kitchen was priceless. She had never met Jackie, but one would never have known that. For the next couple of hours, not one thing was accomplished. Fact is, dinner was an hour later than planned. Mary just couldn't concentrate. Finally, Ray told all of them to stay in the kitchen or they'd never eat.

The phone rang in late afternoon. Nadia answered, "Merry Christmas."

A familiar voice responded, "Hi, Nadia, Merry Christmas to you too."

"Ah, Nate, how did you manage to sneak away?"

"What do you mean?"

"New girlfriend. I'm sure that she's keeping pretty close tabs on you."

"I don't know what you're talking about. There's no new girlfriend and certainly no one at the house."

"Oh, then I guess Carrie's a liar."

"No, she was just mistaken. Anyway, I don't want to fight. I just wanted to wish you and your family a Merry Christmas."

"Thanks, and I'm sorry for my mean comments—totally uncalled for."

"Have you opened your gifts?"

"No, we're a little behind. Jackie surprised us with an early homecoming."

"Wow, that's great! I didn't think she was going to get home until January. Do you have enough snow for snocatting?"

"Oh there's snow. Lots of it. Jackie is beside herself with joy, not having seen snow for two years. She wants to delay opening presents until tomorrow so she can go snocatting right now."

"Is she going to get her way?"

"Not on your life. Snocatting will have to wait until tomorrow—not the presents."

"Would you mind if I called you after church tomorrow?"

"That would be great. Merry Christmas, Nate. Greet your family for us."

"I will. I love you, Nadia."

"Love you too, Nate." The words were spoken before Nadia had time to think about the response. She wondered what that little exchange meant.

The Olsons finally sat down for Christmas Eve dinner. Mary once again had outdone herself. The lutefisk reeked (in Nadia's mind, anyway), but the wonderful aroma of the barbeque ribs permeated the room. The family was complete again and everyone was happy. Ray said grace: "Thank you, Lord, for our good fortune, health, jobs, home, salvation, and especially for the opportunity to be together as a family once again. Thank you for your goodness."

Opening gifts was next on the agenda. Jackie's gifts were the highlight. Each of the women received a beautiful Mother of Pearl ring and the guys got a money clip made by Jackie's Filipino father. Jackie had written a special, personal message on each of the money clips. Both gifts were exquisite.

Kevin and Kate received gifts for their new house. Jackie got mostly clothes. Ginny and Tony had asked for downhill ski equipment, and Nadia received things to improve her golf game, including new golf shoes, which meant that she would no longer have to play in sneakers.

All of the kids had gone together to buy Ray and Mary matching lounge chairs, which they used immediately until they went to bed. The last gifts to be opened came from a big brown box in the basement, filled with gifts, which Kevin explained the UPS man had delivered on the 22nd.

As everyone opened his gift from Nate, Nadia could tell he had spent a lot of time choosing the perfect gift for each individual. He had attached a note to each gift. He gave Jackie clothing with the Twins logo; Ginny and Tony, Kevin and Kate gift certificates to a local furniture store with instructions to pick out something that they would never use their hard-earned money to buy; and Ray an Arctic Cat jacket and pants. Ray's note read: "It amazed me to notice while visiting that your entire family had new and warm clothes for snocatting but you used the clothes you wore for farm work. It's time you look as snappy as the rest of your family, Ray."

Ray loved his gift, but it was Mary's gift that stopped everyone in his tracks. Nate had written: "This gift is for the second most special mother in the world. Enjoy it, Mary, and wear it with pride." In the small box was the most beautiful cross necklace Nadia had ever seen. The diamond in the middle sparkled as Mary took it out of the box put it on her neck. She was touched by Nate's generosity.

The family settled down and waited for Nadia to open her gift. The note taped to the top of the little box read: "Merry Christmas to my favorite farm girl, future LPGA Champion, and someday my wife." She opened the box and picked up a beautiful necklace with a diamond golf ball and gold golf clubs. Inscribed on the shaft were the words: "Love now and forever, Nate."

Nadia loved it, but she felt sad inside, knowing how much she was hurting Nate by not returning his affections. She loved him—no doubt about that—but she wasn't ready to make a commitment. And then there was the "other girl" issue. She wasn't convinced that Nate didn't date other girls. How many times had she wished she would have met him in five years instead of now? She also received a Gortex rain suit and two bestsellers from his parents and Carrie.

The night reminded them of all the wonders of Christmas. They gathered around the fireplace as Mary read the Christmas story from the book of Luke. She closed the Bible and said, "Goodnight and God bless all of you. Pray for peace and salvation throughout the world." Ray and Mary went to bed.

The kids stayed up and visited. It seemed as though they never ran out of things to hash over. Jackie demanded that they catch her up on all the news of the past two years. The conversation invariably turned to Nate.

Nadia said, "He's a good guy, Jackie, and I miss him a lot. The first time he came to visit we were so nervous and we thought Mom was going to have a breakdown. Instead he walked into the house as if he had been here all his life. We've had a few problems but I love him."

Kevin chimed in, "He shoveled cow shit, hauled hay and cleaned the calf pen better than I've ever done. I can't figure out why he's not here."

The conversation went on and on. Nadia felt out-numbered, as if she were drowning and no one would save her. Finally, Ginny came to her rescue. "Listen, if it's meant to be, it will happen; if not, life will go on."

Jackie added her opinion. "Okay, but before it's over, I want to meet this guy. Being the outsider, I would have an unbiased opinion."

Everyone finally submitted to weariness and went to their respective bedrooms. On the way up the stairs Kevin caught up to Nadia. "I love you, Sis."

"I know. I love you too, Kevin."

"I have to tell you, though, I miss Nate. We became good friends."

Santa visited the Olson house as usual. Everyone ran downstairs the next morning, just as they did when they were little kids. They found cameras for the girls and fishing rods for the boys under the Christmas tree. One of the fishing rods remained unopened. The tag read: "To Nate, from Santa."

That Christmas morning the church was filled to capacity. Nadia could understand why even the unchurched—those who never went to church during the year—wanted to go on Christmas. The church was beautifully decorated, and the hymns were always the old favorites, familiar to everyone: "Joy to the World," "Hark the Herald Angels", and "Silent Night."

The four Olson kids were in charge of special music this year. While Ginny was playing the introduction to "O Holy Night," Nadia noticed Nate sitting in the back pew. She hoped they would sound good, and they did. Kevin's base, Ginny's alto, Jackie's high alto, and Nadia's soprano—they all blended perfectly.

When they finished, Kevin almost bowled Nadia over to get off the stage, so he could bring Nate to the rest of the family. Jackie somehow managed to finagle the seat next to Nate. As Pastor Jim invited the congregation to sing the final hymn, he welcomed Nate back to the church and community. "It's always good to have our own Minnesota Twins player in attendance," he said.

It seemed as if everyone in the congregation wanted to greet Nate, so Nadia couldn't even get close to him. After twenty minutes, Ray said, "All aboard, this bus is leaving."

"Go ahead, you guys. I'll jump in with Nate." Kevin gave Katie a quick kiss and ran to join Nate who was already in his car. On the way to the Olson car Jackie said, "That is the best looking man I have ever seen. If he's half as nice as he's good looking, you are nuts not to tie him up and keep him for yourself." She was momentarily distracted from conversation about Nate, but as soon as they pulled into the driveway, she couldn't resist adding, "There must be something wrong with him that I can't see. Or else, I've been away from men too long!"

Nate and Kevin were outside waiting for them when the Olsons pulled up. Nate greeted the family, "Merry Christmas, everyone."

"And the same to you, Nate." Mary spoke for everyone. "It was a wonderful surprise to see you at church this morning."

"Thanks, Mary. You're looking fantastic."

Mary smiled, "I have my entire family with me. How could I feel anything but wonderful?"

Ray gave Nate a hearty welcome and then formally introduced him to Jackie. Finally, Nate made his way over to Nadia. "Merry Christmas," he said quietly, "if this visit poses a problem for you, I'll leave."

"Well, I have to say that it was a shock to see you in church. When did you leave home?"

"I flew from Sioux Falls to Minneapolis and then rented a car."

"You goofball. You'll be sleeping at 6:00 tonight."

She took his hand and they led the troops into the house. Mary and Jackie were in charge of lunch: leftovers, which turned out to be almost as good as last night's meal. They made plans for the next day as they ate. A long, meandering snocat ride would be the first item on the day's agenda. Everyone predicted a beautiful day with temperatures in the mid 30s and light snow.

The plan for the evening, though, was Scrabble. The teams had already been formed. Nate was on Nadia's team and, while they played hard, they came in second to last. A little before midnight, when Nate could hardly keep his eyes open, the suggestion was made that they go to bed. Nadia showed Nate where he'd be sleeping.

"I hope it's okay that we put the rollaway in Kevin's room for you. As you can tell, the house is pretty full."

"Nadia, I'd sleep in the barn if it meant that was the only way I could stay."

Before he got into bed, Nate went back downstairs to give Mary a thank you card from his parents. "Mom loved your quilt. She called it a work of art."

Mary smiled, "I'm glad she liked it so much. I had fun making it."

The next day was everything they'd hoped it would be. Katie had brought up three snocat machines, so there was one for everyone. Mary was snuggled in her "carriage." They took their time on the trail, enjoying the wildlife and stopping for hot chocolate and cookies. When they arrived home—wet and tired—Scrabble seemed to be a logical way to end the day. This time, Nadia and Nate's team did a little better, but at 11:00 Jackie's team was declared the winner.

Nadia and Nate stayed up a little longer. They hadn't had much of a chance to visit. The subject of Seth came up. Nadia was quick to clarify their relationship, "I only met him once. How could there be anything between us?"

Nate grinned, "I know that, but his impression was WOW!"

"Well, I have no interest in Seth or in any other guy, Nate. You know that if I were ready to settle down, I'd marry you tomorrow."

"That makes me feel a little better."

"Then let's go to bed."

"With one another?"

"Funny, real funny."

Nate grinned, "Yeah, I thought you'd say that. Goodnight."

Breakfast the next morning turned out to be a two-hour meal. Jackie told her family about a young man she met in the Peace Corps. His name was John; he was from New York City and planned to become a lawyer. His Peace Corps commitment would be over in February. Jackie got everyone's attention by nonchalantly saying that before John goes back to college, he wants to come to the farm and meet everyone.

The comment wasn't lost on Mary. "Oh my, I could be sewing three wedding dresses!"

Jackie laughed, "It definitely was love at first sight so I'm not going to say no to that, Mom."

Ray leaned back in his chair. "Mary, we might have to add on to the house. Our family is growing faster every day. Now if we could just get Nadia to make a commitment we'd at least know how many to expect around here."

"Dad, stop."

Nate was loving it. "Ray, I can't think of anyone I'd want on my side more than you. Keep it up."

Katie went back home. Ginny had to go into work to replace someone who had called in sick. Nadia and Mary cuddled up in a blanket and read books they had gotten for Christmas. The guys went for a snocat ride, which turned out to be short, since the temperature had dipped to minus fourteen degrees with a wind from the north. Feeling the need for exercise, Nadia urged Buford to go for a run, but he never moved. She sighed—the dog must have more sense than she had.

That evening they made plans for New Years Eve. "Okay then," Nadia said, "we kids will go to Grand Forks for dinner and stay overnight. I've already made reservations for two rooms."

There weren't many dull moments during the week. The guys accomplished a lot in Kevin's house. They hung cabinets and put in all the bathroom fixtures. By the time they left for Grand Forks on New Year's Eve, they were more than a little ready for some fun.

The seven of them had the time of their lives. They made dinner a dress-up occasion and a long, drawn-out affair—over three hours from appetizer to dessert. Nadia thought it was a good thing that Ray wasn't with them; his patience would have worn thin.

At 9:00 the band started playing and they danced the night and year away. After a sojourn in the hot tub, everyone was ready for bed. Nate had to catch an afternoon flight out of Minneapolis so he left Grand Forks early in the morning. They all agreed that it had been a wonderful evening—and a great week.

Both Kevin and Tony asked Nate to be a groomsman at their weddings. He was honored, but said he couldn't give them an answer until he had checked the Twin's schedule.

Part 5

Nadia found the last week of vacation to be quiet. She and Jackie took down the trees and all of the decorations. Kevin and Ray worked on the house, while Mary sewed on the wedding dresses. She had finished Katie's, so Katie got to try it on. Ginny's was nearly completed. Both dresses were exquisite. Everyone marveled at Mary's ability to take different patterns, put them together and create beautiful pieces of clothing. Mary still had two dresses to sew for herself—one for each wedding. With her teaching responsibilities and a commitment to keeping Ray happy, she would be anything but bored over the winter.

Jackie planned to fly to New York on February 7th to meet John's parents. She was filled with excitement and anxiety. She knew very little about John's parents, except that his dad was the Vice President of Uniroyal and his mother was a doctor. From conversations with John, Jackie knew that his parents wanted him to settle down somewhere on the East coast, a likelihood that didn't trouble her but could be a problem for her family.

Nadia left on Sunday. This was to be her last semester of college until she began working toward her Masters. Nate went with his family on a vacation to Scandinavia to visit their relatives in Norway and Sweden. Nadia was invited to go with them, but the timing made it impossible for her to get away.

Winter dragged on and on—not much snow but freezing rain and temperatures. Nadia hated running on the inside track, but the weather permitted no alternative. She celebrated her 20th birthday by going out to dinner with friends, and then spent the rest of the evening making plans to fly to Arizona to play golf with the college team. The coach had made all of the arrangements several weeks ago. She guessed he was eager to see how she scored, and that expectation made her both nervous and excited.

Nadia's flight left on a freezing Monday morning. True to his word, the Arizona coach had sent two members of the team to pick her up at the airport. The two girls and Nadia hit it off immediately. It didn't seem to bother them that this stranger was there to try out for a spot on their team. Both girls had been a part of two championships. One of them, Nan, told Nadia that she would be staying with them.

Tee time was at 10:00 the next day. It was 71 degrees when they woke up and the forecast was for a high of 76. Nadia knew that the pants and long-sleeved shirts she had packed were wrong as soon as she walked into her roommates' kitchen. Nan took her by the hand and when they emerged from the bedroom five minutes later, Nadia was dressed in shorts and a golf shirt.

She wasn't nervous until they walked into the clubhouse. There must have been sixty people standing there. Tom and Sal were front and center with big smiles on their faces. It was comforting to see them. Nadia also recognized the golf pro from the Bahamas. He gave her a thumbs up.

Twelve girls would be playing. Their names were put into a hat. Unfortunately, neither of her roommates was in the foursome with Nadia. A girl named Patty sauntered over and looked Nadia over, "I sincerely hope you don't think that you can come down here and beat one of us, especially being from the Tundra where there's snow on the ground eight months out of the year."

Before Nadia could respond, the girl with whom she was sharing a cart told her to ignore everything Patty said. "She's jealous. You know there has to be one in every group."

After the fifth hole it got very quiet. Nadia had parred three holes and birdied two. After the ninth hole, Patty told the coaches that Nadia was rude and played out of turn. The coaches must have heard her tattling before, however, because they told her to join another foursome, and Nadia's group got Nan.

The back nine was more difficult. Nadia's score was still an impressive 70, which earned a nod of approval from both Sal and Tom.

After the match, all of the girls were excited to leave in order not to be late for a fraternity party. They asked Nadia to join them and she said that she would. Before she left she asked Sal if he would call her parents and let them know how the day went.

"Of course. May I call Nate also?"

Nadia nodded, "Absolutely, as long as it went as well as it did. Tomorrow if I don't play well, we won't tell a soul."

The frat party was a zoo—everyone talking at once, people all over the place, no opportunity for conversation. Nadia hadn't ever experienced that kind of noise level, and she felt uncomfortable with the drinking and smoking. Her roommates had found guys, and the only person in the room she recognized was that of her nemesis, who seemed to be intent on humiliating her. Before Nadia could decide what to do, a couple of guys approached her. Nadia recognized them as Patty's friends.

"What's the matter? Haven't you ever been to a frat party before? Here, have a beer. You don't drink? Everyone drinks." The taunting continued until one of the guys brought over a tall glass and told Nadia to drink it. "It's a fruit smoothie. Drink it or we'll force it down your throat."

Now, Nadia was really scared and she looked for an escape. She saw that the back door had been blocked with furniture. It seemed as if everyone was watching her every move. Patty was busy telling everyone what a hick Nadia was and how she thought that she could just waltz onto the campus and expect everyone to bow down to her because she could hit a golf ball.

Nadia turned to two girls close by. "Would you please get Nan? I really want to go home."

Patty sneered, "Hey, Girl, you're hundreds of miles from home. Don't you ever call this home. Do you understand?"

Nadia started crying. "Please, would someone call a cab for me?"

No one moved. Two of the guys grabbed her as the third one started pouring the drink into her mouth. Nadia was choking and gagging, but all she heard was laughter. They were dragging her up the stairs, all the while arguing about who was going to "do her first." The last thing Nadia remembered was pleading with them not to rape her. They exploded in laughter, and she blacked out.

When Nadia awoke, she was lying in a strange room. Sal, Tom and another man were sitting by the bed. "What happened? My head is splitting." When she realized that the stranger was a police officer, she said to him, "Please tell me they didn't rape me."

Sal spoke first. "Honey, you weren't raped."

"Then, how did you know to come here?"

Sal looked at her and said, "I'm not really sure what made me think you needed us, but Tom and I were sitting around the hotel and all of a sudden this strong feeling that something was wrong came over me. We ran to the parked police car in front of the hotel and told the officer that you were at a huge frat party and that you were in trouble. The officer knew exactly where the party was."

His voice broke, and Nadia had to encourage him to go on. "The officer ran into the house and demanded to know where you were. All of us ran upstairs and started opening up doors—it's a huge house—until we found you. You were unconscious. Tom threw a blanket over you and more policemen entered the room. They handcuffed the three guys and took them to the patrol car. They ordered everyone in the room not to leave."

Nadia looked expectantly at him, "Are you sure they didn't . . . ."

Sal interrupted her, "No, Nadia, they didn't rape you."

Tears rolled down Nadia's eyes. "Thank God," she whispered. Then she went to sleep and slept the rest of the night. When she awoke, Kevin and Nate were both at her bedside. She started crying again.

Nate went to her and took her hand. "Please, Nadia, don't cry. We're going to take you home with us."

"Don't leave me, Nate."

"Not on your life."

After Nadia was discharged, Kevin and Nate took her to the police station so she could give the officer a statement of what happened. On the way in, she bumped into Nan who took her arm. "Nadia, I want . . . ."

Nadia looked at her. "It doesn't matter what you want, you'll never get anything from me. I thought you were my friend, but if you were, you could never have let this happen."

"I wanted to explain. I met someone that night and . . . ."

"Goodbye, Nan." Nadia proceeded into the station with Kevin and Nate. A young female officer greeted her and asked that she come with her—alone. But Nadia wanted Kevin and Nate to be with her, and the officer agreed.

In the room with three officers, Nadia provided the details of her nightmare as well as she could. The meeting took thirty minutes. At the end, they explained to her that she would have to come back and testify at the trial, if it came to that. Nadia had to suppress a tiny amount of skepticism. Sal had told her that one of the guys who assaulted her was the son of a judge, and the chances of him receiving any kind of real punishment were small. But she didn't say anything to the officers, except to assure them that she would be at the trial.

Nadia flew out of Phoenix the next day. Mary was sitting in her dorm room when she arrived, and Nadia was so happy to see her, she couldn't let go when they hugged. Mary had taken a few days off from school to stay with her. She promised Nadia that they would do whatever Nadia wanted to do during the time she was there. And they did have fun. After Nadia told her mother the story, the incident was never brought up again, except for an occasional detail that Nadia wanted to share. They went for pizza, played Rummikub, did a little shopping—Mary even went to a couple of Nadia's classes.

All too soon, it was time for Mary to go, and Nadia was left alone with her thoughts. She filled them with hours of studying and running; the days went by quickly. She received numerous letters from universities, inviting her to try out for their golf team. Nadia glanced at the letters and placed them in a drawer. The memories of her nightmare in Arizona were too fresh; she wasn't interested in any kind of change.

She turned in her thesis the day it was due. Even though she felt that it was good—having spent countless hours researching and writing—Nadia was nervous because it counted so much toward her final grade.

The Twins were due back in town for their first home game on April 13th. Team members had worked hard and left spring training with a winning record. Nate told Nadia that notes hung in the dressing rooms of all players, asking the question "What went wrong in October?"

Nate had been a rock for Nadia. The Twins management had bent over backwards to allow him to travel to Arizona and then Minneapolis when he thought she needed him. He had also alerted the management to the upcoming trial—somewhat anxiously because he thought that there might be some threat to his contract renewal. However, that never came to pass, and his contract was renewed when the time came.

Most of the time, the weather was beautiful with spring-like temperatures in the low 70s. Even though the weather was nice, the Twins began the season with a few indoor games, which Nadia attended when she could but hated it because baseball was meant to be played outdoors. She waited for Nate after the games, and enjoyed the dinners she attended with the other players and their wives. Nadia felt good about Nate and their relationship and looked forward to spending more time with him.

As if reading Nadia's mind, Nate called Kevin and Tony to tell them that it was a go for him and their weddings. Concerned about the phone bill, Nadia had to insist that he hang up after forty five minutes.

Nate was unapologetic. "I really like your brother and Tony too. When we get married would you consider living at the farm?"

Nadia smiled. "And pray, tell me, what would you do there? There aren't too many professional baseball teams in Northern Minnesota."

"Wasn't thinking about playing baseball. No, I think I'd become a farmer—maybe coach baseball."

"Sounds good to me. I just hope you're young enough when you retire to still possess the energy and strength needed to run a farm. Farming is tough work."

"How does four years from now sound?"

"How about if we wait and see what the next four years bring?"

Nadia enjoyed the bantering. She knew that she loved Nate. What she didn't know was when she would be ready to make the marriage commitment. Nate seemed so sure of himself and his ability to make that commitment.

Sal called and asked Nadia to join him for a Sunday game. When she met him, she inquired about Sandy's absence. Sal explained that Sandy had to stay in Florida because she was busy with yet another project that required her presence. Nadia asked Sal about the project, and he shook his head in obvious admiration for his wife.

According to Sal, Sandy was shopping at a mall, and was waiting in line to pay for her purchases. Ahead of her were a young woman and two children. The woman was trying to pay for her clothes, but she was short of money. The cashier was loud and obnoxious, "What do you mean you don't have another forty cents?"

Instead of arguing, the woman took the children's hands and walked out. Sandy paid for the woman's merchandise, left her own things on the counter, and ran out of the store. She caught up to the woman and gave her the bag. Then she walked back into the store and asked to speak to the manager. The cashier muttered something like "I don't care if I am fired; people shouldn't shop if they don't have the money."

Sandy then noticed the young woman sitting by the fountain with her two young children close by, quietly reading a book. When Sandy sat down, the woman told her that her husband had been killed by a stray bullet in a drive-by shooting. She worked at an insurance company full time, but the money was tight and she couldn't get any assistance for the children unless she quit her job. She made it clear that she didn't want to be on welfare.

Then Sal laughed. "And wouldn't you know it, Sandy asked if she could take them on a shopping spree, which she did. She accompanied them home, and the woman invited her in for coffee. When Sandy left, she went to the apartment manager and paid the rent for six months. Said that she hadn't had so much fun in a long time."

And so *Helping Her* was born. Sal told Nadia that, with every one of Sandy's "projects", he sees less and less of her. He laughed when he said that Seth had come up with a new name for his grandmother's compassion—Inheritance Spent. Sal's love for Sandy was obvious, and Nadia was comforted by the fact that two people could still be in love after so many years of marriage.

After several home games, Nate flew to Denver for a series. A few days after he left, Nadia was informed that she would graduate magna cum laude. Her advisor called to congratulate her and told her that he had enjoyed reading her thesis. "You did an excellent job of researching the topic and writing about it. The people you have chosen to work with in your career are fortunate to have you." His words made Nadia feel good about her career choice and her hard work of the last four years.

May and June were busy months with graduation, two weddings, and farming responsibilities. Ray hired two men to help with the farm work in anticipation of the busy days ahead. When Nadia inquired about his decision, he laughed.

"Well, it doesn't take a rocket scientist to figure out that I won't be able to do all of the farm work in addition to the jobs your mother has in mind for me. I just hope the weather cooperates and our crops are good so we can pay the men's salaries. So you'll be home for the summer?"

Nadia shook her head. "I don't think so, Dad. I'm going to start working on my Masters Degree. In fact, as soon as I get back to Minneapolis, I'm going to check up on the classes I'll need so I can divide them up and graduate in a year and a half."

Her father looked concerned. "I don't know if that's a good idea. You'll stretch yourself too thin."

"But you know how easy school is for me, Dad. I can do this."

"Just make sure that you leave time to rest. By the way, have you gained any weight? It doesn't look as if you have."

"A couple of pounds. I'm not running very much these days. What I need is a week of Mom's cooking."

Nadia loved talking with her Dad. He always made her feel good and very much loved.

When Nadia arrived back at the dorm the next day, a surprise was waiting for her. Sitting on her couch were Ginny and Katie who, Nadia discovered, just decided they needed to get away. Nadia was happy to see them and made sure that they knew they were going to stay with her for as long as they could.

They enjoyed a fabulous four days together, starting with the consumption of a huge box filled with goodies from Mary: cookies, bars, homemade bread, jam, pears, peaches, peas and carrots. They ate it all in between shopping sprees and movies. It was all such fun, and Nadia was sorry to see Katie and Ginny leave.

The letter from the Arizona court finally arrived. All three of her attackers had pled guilty, and Nadia was ordered to appear in court on May 2nd. She called home with the news and learned that most of the plans for the trial had been made some time ago. Kevin would be going with her, as would Sal and Tom, who were required to testify also. Sal would take care of the plane tickets, and everyone would be on the same flight. Once again, Nadia sent a prayer upward, thanking God for family and friends.

For the next few days, Nadia worked hard on a speech that her advisor asked her to give to fellow graduate students on her thesis. He wanted her to describe her field research about children who suffer mentally and physically and have been ignored by society in some way. Nadia was happy to accept. She loved children, and she had no trouble talking about the importance of their need for love, safety and good homes.

Kevin arrived at the dorm the night before they were to leave. "The housekeeper would have a cardiac if she knew I was sneaking a good looking man to my room," Nadia said.

"No need to worry. Sal called to tell us he was coming to pick both of us up. We'll stay at their house. You know, Sis, if the circumstances were different, I'd be looking forward to this trip. I talked to Nate just before I left home. He wants to be there for you."

"I know, Kevin, but he needs to play ball so he can save up free time for the weddings."

They all enjoyed shrimp scampi at a popular restaurant and went over the next day's agenda with the attorney that Sal had hired as they ate. He told Nadia that he had spoken with the attorneys who were representing her attackers, and reassured her that she had nothing to worry about.

On the plane the next morning, Nadia was delighted to see Sandy who decided to join them at the last minute. Sandy explained how her life had changed once she realized that money wouldn't buy her happiness.

"Now, God is number one, family number two and helping as many people as possible is number three. Nadia, after you get your Masters, let's start a nationwide campaign for a better life for women and their children."

Nadia could hardly contain herself. "This is incredible. That is exactly one of my goals."

Sandy looked at her. "I hope that your goals also include marrying Nate."

Nadia assured her that Nate was somewhere on the list. She was feeling increasingly anxious as the plane taxied to the gate.

Sandy suggested they have lunch before they went to court, but Nadia's stomach was in knots and lunch would be a bad idea. They went directly to the courthouse, arriving at 12:30. At 12:45 the door opened and in walked Nate. Nadia flew out of her chair and held onto him for dear life.

"I love you, Nate. I love you so much."

"I love you too, Nadia. That's why I'm here."

At 1:00 sharp the bailiff came and ushered them into the courtroom. Nadia looked straight ahead as she walked past the three guys. The judge announced the counts against each of them and asked them how they wanted to plead. They all pled guilty to the charge. Then they were given a chance to speak. Sam, the son of a judge, stood up.

"I have been asked to speak on behalf of all of us. Nadia, we are sorry . . . ." Most of the rest of his speech was difficult to understand because there were so many tears and nose blowing. He ended with a statement that Nadia knew came from his heart.

"Please look at me for just this last minute. I know it is hard to believe that something good could possibly come out of this horrendous situation, but it has. I have become a different person, someone I've actually wanted to be for years. Every day when I wake up I ask myself, 'What can you do today to make a difference in someone's life?' and I've followed through with it. There are thousands of people who need love and help and if I can make a difference in just a few of those lives, I will consider my life a success. We are all sorry for what we put you through. Each of us sitting here today is ready to accept our punishment. Please forgive us. Thank you."

The judge turned to her. "Nadia, before I hand out the sentences, would you care to say something?"

"Thank you, Your Honor. I want to say that I've forgiven all of you. What happened that evening is something I want to forget about and the only way it is possible is to forgive you. I pray that this truly will be a life-changing experience for all of you. We are young, healthy and blessed. Make a difference in your world. Thank you."

They were all sentenced to 350 hours of community service. The judge was firm. "Your service will begin on June 1st and be completed by August 30th. You will be supervised at all times and will divide your time among the following places: the three downtown missions and the two homes for abused children, Teen Challenge and the Big Brother/Big Sisters headquarters, where each one of you will adopt a child for the summer. Have I made myself perfectly clear?"

They spoke in unison, "Yes, Your Honor."

The next few minutes were awkward. Nadia wanted to get out of there. She had accepted their apologies and said what she wanted to say. Now it was over, done with, and never to be brought up again.

The next few minutes she had with Nate were precious. "I'm so glad and thankful that this is over."

They all rode to the airport together. Nate flew to Tampa Bay and the rest to Minneapolis. Kevin and Nadia stayed at Sal's that night and returned to their respective homes in the morning.

Kevin looked at Nadia. "Finally, we we'll be able to focus on all the fun events in our lives. Take care of yourself and put on a few pounds. Love you, Sis."

"Love you too, Big Brother, and thank you from the bottom of my heart."

A ton of bricks had been lifted from Nadia's shoulders. She called her parents to let them know that Kevin had just left. She didn't want to talk about what happened; she knew that Kevin would fill them in. Mary detected a difference in Nadia's voice. "You sound like your old self," she said.

"I am, Mom, and I'm ready to enjoy this summer. I love you both so much and I'll see you in less than two weeks. I can't believe that I'm graduating! Oh wait, Mom, should I make hotel reservations for you?"

"Nope, we already have them. Bye Sissy." Her Mom hadn't called her by that name for years. Nadia felt warm and fuzzy when she crawled into bed.

Nadia's English professor had agreed to meet with her to go over her speech which she wanted to be perfect. She was pleased when her professor gave it his stamp of approval. "I would not change one word of this. It's very well-written, and if you present it with the conviction you have in your heart, it will be great. I'll try to be there when you give it."

Nate checked in every day. The Twins played at home on Thursday, Friday and Saturday. On Sunday, Nate and Nadia went for a bike ride and picnic by the Falls. The Twins were now well over the 500 mark, but the jokes about last year just wouldn't quit. The sports channels continually reminded the viewers not to worry about the Twins. They said things such as, "Even if the Twins win every game during the regular season, they'll fold in October." The sarcasm made a fan like Nadia sick to her stomach.

Nadia wished that graduation would be held on another weekend so Nate could be there, but it was not going to happen. The Twins had to be in St. Louis on Thursday night.

Jackie and her friend John flew in on Thursday. Nadia picked them up at the airport. After the formal introductions were over, Nadia blurted out, "Wow, we Olson girls certainly have the ability to find the best looking men!"

John grinned, "Thanks, I accept the compliment."

The three of them had a great time. They enjoyed dinner at Josie's, compliments of John's parents. John ordered all of them an after dinner drink: Bailey's—on the rocks. Nadia decided that it was like drinking a chocolate malt. "It's really too good," she said, "Maybe I shouldn't have tried it."

They were going to take a cab to the hotel, but Nadia convinced them to let her drive them. When she asked the name of the hotel, she was taken aback to learn that it was the downtown Hilton. "How in the world can Mom and Dad afford rooms for all of us at that place?" She was perplexed and sad when she thought of all the money her parents were spending for the weekend. As late as it was, she decided to call Nate.

"I'm upset, Nate. Mom and Dad got rooms at the Hilton for everyone. I just dropped off Jackie and John. Nate, they can't afford this."

"Honey, I don't know what to do. I'm hundreds of miles away."

By Friday at 4:00, everyone was gathered in the hotel lobby with no specific plans. It was raining cats and dogs, so they decided to go to Ray and Mary's room on the 22nd floor.

Nadia gave her parents a hug. "Mom and Dad, there are only two suites on this whole floor. What were you thinking?"

"This is a special occasion," Mary replied, "and we wanted everything to be perfect."

Hot tub, game table, TV screen the size of a movie theater, cheese and fruit trays—you name it, it was all there. At 6:00 the phone rang. Mary announced that dinner would be served at 7:00 in the Black Raven restaurant downstairs. It was at this point that Nadia knew her parents did not set all this up. "Mom, who's doing this?"

"I'll give you three guesses and the first two don't count."

"Nate."

"Yes, we tried to tell him this wasn't necessary, but you know Nate, only the best for his farm girl."

"Mom, I want him here so badly."

"Are you two any closer to making wedding plans?"

"Not you too. I've got to get done with college; then I'm sure we'll set the date."

"I think that Jackie and John will beat you to the altar. Dad and I were talking about how lucky we are. We have four wonderful children and soon will be blessed with four wonderful sons-and daughters-in-law."

Dinner was a culinary delight: Caesar salad, French Onion soup, filet mignon that was so tender no steak knife was necessary, Au Gratin potatoes, sliced carrots, and cheesecake for desert.

Nadia thought that Katie and Ginny drank a little too much wine, since they both kept singing show tunes and laughing. She excused herself at 10:00 so she could talk to Nate.

"You goofball," she said as soon as she heard his voice, "Why did you spend all this money? You're probably playing these two games just to pay for our fun. And it has been fun. Even Dad has to admit he enjoyed the dinner."

Nate told Nadia that he had asked her folks to videotape the graduation for him. "Do a good job, now. I wish I could be there to celebrate with everyone. I love you."

The ceremony didn't start until 2:00 but by 1:30 there wasn't a seat left in the auditorium. Nadia was glad that her family along with Sal, Sandy, Seth, Tom, Gloria and Carrie were all sitting in the front row. She had memorized her speech, but was still worried about getting stage fright.

She needn't have been afraid. Nadia's speech got a standing ovation. She couldn't have asked for a more delightful response from the audience, and she took its enthusiasm as a sign of support for her career.

Nadia received a few gifts at the little party her family and friends had for her afterward. Her favorite gift of all was from John's parents who enclosed a copy of the check they had sent to a shelter for abused children in New York City.

The time came when everyone said goodbye and headed home. Sal and Sandy left first, followed by Kevin, Katie, Ginny and Tony. Nadia stayed so she could take Jackie and John to the airport. Both of them had jobs in New York for the summer. In the fall, Jackie would begin working at The University of Michigan in the foreign language department, while John would take the bar exam and pursue a job with a law firm in Ann Arbor. John promised Nadia that he would work on setting up a fund for abused children. Nadia was grateful for his expertise in the financial department.

Part 6

On the drive home Nadia thought about all of the things that would have to be done before the weddings. There was a lot to do and not much time, since the weddings were only ten days away. Nadia knew that her job would be the yard. Mary was confident that with Nadia in charge, there wouldn't be a weed in the garden or a blade of grass out of place.

When Nadia arrived home she looked around and was amazed at the number of things that had already been done. Kevin and Ray had turned the part of the pasture that was closest to the yard into a parking lot. Flower pots were already in place in the yard to make the aisle for the wedding party. A white arbor was placed just outside the front door where the couples would make their entrance. A huge tent was cleverly hidden in the backyard—up and ready for service just in case Mother Nature didn't cooperate.

The weekend of the weddings dawned warm and sunny. The guests began arriving on Thursday, right before an old-fashioned wiener roast Mary and Ray hosted that evening—hot dogs, baked beans, potato salad, chips and s'mores. Sal told Kevin that he never thought anything could taste so good.

The outside rehearsal was at 8:00 that evening. Nate couldn't get there until 9:30 so they had to have a rerun for him. The guys were chomping at the bit. Kevin and Tony had rented rooms in the neighboring town and it was time to have a little fun. What "fun" meant was left to Nadia's imagination.

The Olson women woke up the next morning to a beautiful sunrise. All twelve of the girls were staying at Katie's house, including eight bridesmaids for the double June weddings. As maids of honor, Jackie and Nadia felt responsible for their happiness, and today their job was to get all of them excited for the afternoon softball game.

Katie sighed, "I wish I knew what kind of shape our future husbands and their friends are in."

Jackie, in her characteristic smart aleck way, responded, "No, I feel that we are better off not knowing the gory details. I don't know much of what John had planned along with the rest of them, but I'm pretty sure that tea and crumpets weren't a part of the plan. With that bit of information, do you still want to speculate on how they're feeling?"

Nadia agreed with Jackie. "I guess that's the reason for a Thursday night dress rehearsal, instead of right before the wedding. At least they'll have today to sleep and regain consciousness."

Mary meandered over to Katie's house at 10:30. "I certainly hope you had fun last night. Dad and I were in bed at 10:00, bored to death. He wanted to be with the guys and I wanted to be with you girls." She tried to look sad, but broke out laughing instead. "Actually, the bed felt very good."

Teams for the softball game had already been determined. Katie's and Tony's friends and family were pitted against the Olson clan.

"How unfair is that having Nate on your team," complained Katie.

Nadia laughed, "It may be a disadvantage, actually. I can't wait to see how he hits a ball that's thrown four times slower than what he's used to."

Twelve thirty and the yard filled up with people. The weather was cooperating. Five minutes before game time the guys showed up, seemingly no worse for the wear.

Nate yelled out a greeting. "Hello everybody! See, I got everyone up and ready by game time."

Jackie wasn't impressed. "What a man! John, what time did you go to bed?"

"Hey, what happened last night stays with us. Maybe a few years from now, you'll hear the details, but not now, and surely not from us."

Mary, forever the peacemaker, asked, "Are any of you hungry?"

Kevin shook his head. "No, we had breakfast brought in. All we want to do now is play ball. Let's go!"

Borrowed bleachers from the school were filling up. Ray handed out red t-shirts to the Olson team, blue to the in-laws, and white to all the fans. It was a pretty impressive sight!

Nate snuggled up to Nadia. "Are you ready for this? We're under a lot of pressure. You know we're expected to win."

It was awesome to have him there. Nadia wondered who she should thank for excusing Nate from playing—allowing him to miss a game.

"Let the game begin." Sal was the official umpire behind the plate. Tom was his assistant.

There couldn't have been many people left in town, judging from the number that came out for the family game. One thing you have to say about small towns: people love any kind of special entertainment. There must have been 350 townspeople, either playing or cheering. After nine innings, no one wanted to quit playing, that is, until the catering vans pulled in the driveway. At that point, the game ended abruptly. People were hungry, as was evidenced by the consumption of every morsel of food on the table. With not a scrap of food lying around anywhere, Buford resigned himself to taking a nice nap under the tree.

One of the guys yelled, "Nite Lite Golf at 10:00 for anyone who wants to play or, should we say, has the energy to play."

Kevin shook his head, "I don't know—maybe we should cancel tonight's activities. I'm exhausted and I'm young."

"No, Kevin," Nadia said, "we can't cancel. Let's go there and if no one shows up, we'll go home."

Much to their surprise, the clubhouse was packed with 70 eager participants, so the game was on. Everyone had a good time until midnight, when Tony strongly suggested that it was time to go home. Sal reluctantly agreed with him. "I don't know when I've had a better time. I feel sorry for the next family that plans a wedding in this town—has quite an act to follow!"

The next morning dawned similar to the last two—sunny and warm. Nadia jumped out of bed when Mary tiptoed into her room. "Sorry, Mom, I should have been up earlier to help you."

"No need. Your father made sure this weekend would be a time for us to have fun. I feel kind of worthless myself. Look outside, it's absolutely breathtaking!"

Nadia glanced out the window. Everything was in place—flowers, arches, tables, chairs, candelabras, the wedding party platform—and, best of all, the sun was shining. Nadia loved it all. "It's so beautiful, Mom."

Just then Ray walked in the house and they sat down to a breakfast of oatmeal and toast. Nadia left to join the rest of the girls at Katie's house to get ready for the wedding. They had all decided that there would be no beauty shop hairdos—just natural.

Nate sneaked over at noon. He gave Nadia a big hug and then was pushed out of the house by Jackie who was monitoring the time. "Get back to the guys. You can be with her later."

To say that the wedding was spectacular is an understatement. The bridesmaids wore long dresses in the palest rose with a shade darker for the maids of honor. The guys all wore black pants, white shirts and ties that matched the dresses. Ginny and Katie looked perfect. The whole wedding was like one you read about in a fairy tale. More food than Nadia had ever seen in one place was consumed. There was dancing late into the night, but finally the wedding couples got into their respective cars and left in a barrage of honking horns and cheering fans. Soon they were gone, and the wedding was over.

For a few minutes after the last guest had left, the Olsons gathered in the kitchen. John was the first to suggest that bed sounded good. "I never thought a weekend on the farm could be so exhausting."

Nadia couldn't remember a Sunday when the family hadn't gone to church, but it happened on this weekend. Even Mary didn't get up until later in the morning. Ray, as exhausted as he was, however, had no choice but to get up and feed the cattle. He was sleeping in his chair when the rest of the family started moving around.

One glance outside and Nadia wondered if a double wedding with 400 guests had actually taken place last night. The yard looked like it did four days ago except for a little padded down grass where people had danced and partied. Who could have cleaned everything up so quickly? And how much did these weddings cost her parents anyway? Maybe she and Nate would run off and get married and then come home to tell everyone. Hopefully, Ray and Mary would have time to pay the bills before Jackie and John's wedding.

Nate, Nadia, Jackie and John spent four quiet, peaceful hours on the lake. They fished, swam and soaked in the sun. The clouds starting rolling in about 5:00 and a couple of hours later, it was pouring rain. But no one cared. Now that the weddings were over, the rain could fall. The weather gods had been good to them when they needed it. They played Rumikub the rest of the evening.

On Monday morning Nate, John and Jackie left. Nadia planned to leave around noon. Mary was already lamenting an empty house once again, but deep in her heart, Nadia thought that she was probably looking forward to some peace and quiet. The newlyweds would be arriving home later in the week after separate honeymoons to South Dakota and Canada, and then it would be back at work and school as usual.

Having played five games in six days, Nate hadn't been able to spend much time with Nadia on the farm. But all of the hard work paid off, because the Twins made it to the final series. Maybe this would be their year.

Katie, Kevin, Ginny, Tony and Nadia all went to the first game of the World Series in Minneapolis. The Twins were victorious over the Yankees, 8-6, and went on to win another game, 4-3. The Twins flew out immediately after the second game. The Olson contingent gave Nate strict orders: "Win those games in New York so we can be part of the celebration in Minneapolis."

Nate was solemn. "Anything for you guys. Love you, Nadia."

Back on the farm, Kevin and Katie's home became a "baseball stadium." Everyone's schedule revolved around the games in New York. Almost without realizing what was happening, the Olsons and thousands of other fans watched in horror as the Yankees walloped the Twins in both games. It was déjà vu. Could it be happening again, Nadia wondered?

Nadia begged Ray and Mary to go with them to Minneapolis for the last game, but her parents refused, even with the promise of prime seats, compliments of Nate. "No, you kids go; your mother and I will enjoy the game in the comfort of our living room." Ray added, "Besides, we won't have to deal with the crowds and we'll get to watch the replays."

They all arrived at Nate's house at 11:00 on the day of the big game, but Nate wasn't there to greet them. He was staying at a hotel with the team. Kevin couldn't contain his enthusiasm when he spotted a new red car in the driveway. "Wow, guess who got a new car! It must be nice to be rich!"

He had to change his tune when Nadia brought him a note that Nate had left, telling them to make themselves at home and rest up so they could cheer at the game. Then Kevin read the rest of the note: "Hope you like your new car, Farm Girl. It's ready to go—insurance paid for and a full gas tank. See you at the game."

Before Nadia could process the surprise, the phone rang and Kevin answered, "Hello, you've reached the home of baseball's MVP. How can we help you?"

There was laughter at the other end. Nadia knew it was Nate. She took the phone from Kevin. "Nate, you can't keep spoiling me like this. The car is beautiful though! Yes, we'll be ready when a limo picks us up tomorrow. Ten o'clock is fine. See you then. Love you too."

"Yay!" Katie yelled from the other room. "I hated the idea of looking for a parking place. A limo—wow! Life is gooooooood . . . ."

The scene at the stadium was beyond description—so many people milling around that it was difficult getting inside. Game time was an hour away and every seat was filled. The Olsons took their seats directly behind the catcher. Pandemonium broke out as the Twins came out on the field. Nate looked towards them and grinned when he caught Nadia's eye. Nadia mouthed the words, "Love you. Play well."

After a seemingly long time of stretching, hitting balls and running—all with the backdrop of a cheering crowd—the Twins left the field and the Yankees replaced them. There was a lot less cheering from the Twins fans, but not much booing either. It was a time to relax the old vocal cords.

Nine innings of amazing baseball ended with a 6-6 tie. Nadia felt the exhaustion of the players from both teams. They held one another scoreless for the next three innings, and then Nate came up to bat. It was the bottom of the 13th with two outs and no one on base. Within seconds, the count was two and three. The sixth pitch was released; the result sounded like gunfire. Nate flew around the bases and slid into home plate. The Twins were the World Series Champions, and the love of Nadia's life was the hero!

The noise was deafening. The players and fans climbed on Nate until Nadia couldn't see him. She was terrified that he was being crushed. He finally emerged from the pile and motioned for Nadia to come over.

"No way," Nadia yelled. "I feel safe standing here."

Nate insisted. "The players' wives and kids are all down here. Join us."

She went down, just as a layer of calm descended upon the stadium. Then she heard the announcement: "Ladies and gentlemen, the World Series Champions, our Minnesota Twins!" There were literally thousands of flashes from around the stadium. Nadia had never felt prouder.

The team left the field to continue the celebration in the locker room, while the fans celebrated outside on the streets of Minneapolis.

The Olsons arrived back at Nate's, just as he drove up. More celebration followed—too much. Nadia had no idea when the men decided to call it a night, but the next morning, when the chimes rang eleven times and there was still no sign of life in any of them, she knew that the celebration had continued far into the night. Tony finally got up and roused the others. As they made their way to the pickup, Tony groaned, "This is one time I wish I were independently wealthy. I wonder what the school would say if I called in sick the next two days."

Kevin retorted, "Not a chance. If Katie and I have to work, so do you. Besides, your job wasn't easy to come by, so you'd better not jeopardize it."

Nadia hated to see her family leave. She had decided to stay and join the "Twins family" for the parade. An hour later, the house filled up again. Tom and Gloria, Sal and Sandy and several people Nadia had never met came over. By 8:00 she wanted to go to bed and was not unhappy when Sal told everyone that it was time to go home.

The following two days were pretty much the same: house to house gatherings filled with food, drinks, and chatter. She was happy when Wednesday morning arrived and she could go home to the farm where peace and quiet were the norm.

Nate was chosen MVP. It wasn't a surprise to anyone. He decided to make a visit to the farm, because all he really wanted at this point was some of Mary's good home-cooked meals and relaxation. He wasn't an attention-getter, and the only way to not attract attention was to leave. He couldn't even put gas in his pickup without being mobbed.

The week on the farm was everything he wanted and needed. Ray and Mary had a small party so their friends would have a chance to congratulate the hero. Other than that, Nate hauled bales and helped Kevin and Ray clean up the machinery and get it put away for the winter.

The Olsons enjoyed another Thanksgiving and Christmas. They were once again thankful for health, warm homes, lots of snow and one another.

Nate invited Nadia's entire family to join his family in Daytona Beach for New Years. The Olsons eagerly anticipated the warm temperatures and a few days of relaxation. They enjoyed a New Year's Eve dinner at an exquisite restaurant. As dessert was being served, the band began playing "The Rose," Nadia's all-time favorite song. Nate got up from his chair, knelt down next to Nadia, and said, "Nadia, will you marry me?"

Without missing a beat, Nadia said, "You bet! Yes, yes, yes, Nate, I'll marry you."

The band immediately began playing "Happy Days." Nate placed a beautiful solitaire diamond on Nadia's finger. Ray was the first to speak. "Welcome to our family, Nate. I was hoping this would take place before I got so old and senile I wouldn't know what was happening."

The rest of the vacation was almost as wonderful as that moment. Not one minute was wasted indoors. Everyone looked amazingly healthy as they stepped back into reality a week later in Minneapolis where it was 18 degrees below zero with a north wind whipping at 20 miles per hour. Jackie and John headed east. John had proposed at Thanksgiving so both of them were deep into wedding plans.

A new semester of school started for Nadia. She threw herself into studying, so that her plans to graduate after the summer session would materialize.

Nate spent more time at the farm that winter than anywhere else. He purchased some land next to the lake and about five miles from the farm. Kevin and Tony were becoming increasingly important to him. At the same time, Ginny and Katie were getting bigger every day. They seemed to be in a constant state of exuberance over their pregnancies. Katie was due in April and Ginny in May. It was ironic how they were married at the same time, and now they were celebrating their expanding stomachs together!

Nate had signed another two-year contract with the Twins, and left for spring training in Florida in the middle of March. He and Nadia planned to be married a year from Christmas. They agreed to wait until then so Nadia could graduate and find a job.

Things kept happening in the Olson family. Kassie Olson was born on April 15th and Carrie Crow on May 1st. The two tiny, blonde, blue-eyed angels were welcomed by everyone. Other events included Nadia's graduation in August; the Twins' superb baseball luck; another year of bountiful crops on the farm; Mary's retirement; and the completion of Jackie's wedding plans.

After several weeks of job hunting and interesting interviews, Nadia accepted a position as a social worker with Hennepin County. She made sure that she had one last sojourn on the farm before she joined the ranks of the employed.

The Twins ended up losing the American League Champions series. They were disappointed but not crushed. They had had a wonderful season and all the players would be returning next year.

Nadia and Nate celebrated Thanksgiving in South Dakota with his family and then Christmas on the farm. Nate stayed at the farm for a few more days of snocatting and ice fishing after Nadia left. They spent New Year's Eve together back in Minneapolis.

Nadia loved her job but it kept her confined and unable to be "hands on" with the people she served. She wanted to be on the streets, helping them to achieve a better life.

"My Way" was born in the spring. Nadia and John had worked for hours and hours on getting the financial end set up, including obtaining a non-profit status. Nadia had a tremendous support system, beginning with her family and church families in both her home town and Minneapolis. Nate and his family, as well as Sal and Sandy, were also supportive. It didn't take Nadia long to realize three truths: One should never give cash to a needy person; she had the ability to realize who really wanted to change his life; and there were hundreds of people who needed help, but they didn't know where to start.

Nadia's organization became well known at the food banks located in the Cities that were always running out of food, clothing and shelter. Nadia found money for the Missions which were always filled to capacity especially during the winter months. She was determined that no family would ever have to worry about spending a freezing night outdoors, and she worked overtime to collect food, toys and clothing. She helped with the washing and preparing the items for the people who needed them the next day. She never knew if she would be home at 6:00, 8:00 or midnight; in Nadia's mind, it didn't matter, however, since this was to be her life for a year.

Nate was waiting for her when she arrived home one evening at 8:30. He held out his hand with the box containing Nadia's engagement ring. "What the hell is this all about?" he demanded.

His intensity shocked Nadia. She said, "I never wear my ring when I'm working. Don't you realize how ridiculous it would look if I had a five-carat ring on my finger while I was talking to someone who didn't know where his next meal was coming from?"

Nate shook his head. "Nadia, you don't have to preach to me about the importance of helping people. I grew up in a home where both my parents gave their time and money, remember? I just don't understand why you feel compelled to spend all of your time at your job."

Nadia was dumbfounded. "All of a sudden this comes up? You have known for years that helping people is my passion. You play baseball and it fulfills you; helping people fulfills me. If you can't accept this, well, standing in front of you is the whole package. I love you, but I can't stop doing my job."

"How long are you going to do this?" Nate sounded defiant.

"Do what?"

"Leave the house before sunup and not get home until sundown."

"You know the answer to that question. We had an agreement, remember? You're going to play one more year of baseball, and I'm going to dedicate that year to my work."

Nate looked at her. "I don't know, Nadia. I just don't know."

"Well, I do know. Make a decision now: either you need to accept me for who I am or let me go. It's just that simple."

"You mean you would end everything between the two of us?"

"The choice is yours, Nate, not mine."

The next morning, Nate was nowhere to be found, but a note was lying on the table. It was short and to the point: "I can't live like this. I want you to be with me. I don't know. You make the decision."

Nadia packed up the few things she called her own and hauled them in the car. Then she went apartment hunting.

All she knew after a morning of perusing the newspaper ads and visiting a couple of apartment complexes was that apartments were expensive. She decided to go to work and look at some more afterwards. As badly as her morning had begun, Nadia was glad that she had gone to work because the day definitely got better. A young mother with two children had been living at one of the Missions for weeks. She had applied for dozens of jobs, and yesterday her hard work paid off—she got a job at a bank downtown. The staff convinced her to remain at the Mission for awhile, until Nadia could help her find an apartment.

Nadia delivered vouchers to six food banks. Money wasn't a problem; people were extremely generous. What worried her was the possibility that the generosity wouldn't continue—people would stop giving when they felt they had done their part. She decided to write a letter to all of her support groups to give them an update and show how their financial help had been disseminated. Maybe when they saw the figures on paper, they wouldn't be tempted to stop their giving.

She left downtown at 5:00 so that she could find someplace to live. On a whim, she stopped at a small apartment complex and found, to her a delight, that there was an efficiency apartment available. It had a stove and fridge; she'd have to buy a couch with a pull-out bed, a table and chairs, and a dresser. She paid the deposit and the first month's rent.

Nadia realized that she had left her box of checks and some papers in the top drawer of her dresser at Nate's. She was glad that she still had her keys, so she could get in and out before Nate came home. On the way there, she made a mental note to call home and offer some lame excuse as to why she would be hard to reach for a while. Life can change so quickly.

As Nadia drove into the driveway of her five-bedroom, two-story house with a three-car garage, reality hit her like a rock. Her new home was a one-bedroom apartment, and she had better get used to the change.

Nate scared her as he emerged from the bedroom. He looked horrible, and Nadia couldn't help but feel sorry for him. She said, "Sorry, I didn't think you'd be home, or I would have knocked. I forgot some stuff in the dresser. It will take just a minute."

Nate looked incredulous. "You really are leaving me, aren't you?"

"I don't have a choice, do I? I have a life just like you, and I'm going to live it. Nate, you made this decision for both of us. I think that you have made a huge mistake and you will regret it. By the way, why aren't you in Toronto?"

"I don't know, Nadia. I lose the love of my life and you don't think it should affect me at all?"

"Oh, grow up!"

She left the house and found a phone booth so she could call home. Unfortunately, Kevin answered. It would have been easier to talk to Mary or Ray. After a ten-minute conversation, she went home and allowed herself to cry.

Work consumed Nadia's every minute. An inner city organization was working with her to bring four special concert performances to the city. Every year, these entertainers traveled the world giving concerts, but only the wealthy could afford to attend. By week's end "My Way" had signed contracts with three groups. They would perform for the missions, free of charge with the exception of travel expenses. Nadia planned to hire busses and drivers to pick up parents, teens and children who lived in the underprivileged areas. They would arrive early enough to be guaranteed great seats. Every time something positive like this occurred, Nadia sent out letters to her supporters.

She checked in at the food banks and the Mission to make sure there would be enough food and clothing to carry them through a few days. Satisfied with what she saw and heard, she drove out of the city and headed north. A few days on the farm would do her a world of good.

Summer was coming to an end. What promised to be a perfect few months ended up being a nightmare without Nate. On a more positive note, the Twins were having another banner year; every home game was sold out.

The "Fab 5" of the Olson family decided they would keep their plans intact to go to the last home series. Where they would all stay was the big question. Nate had phoned Kevin to ask them to go ahead with their plans to stay at his house. "Things are shaky between Nadia and me at this time, but my friendship with you guys will never change."

Shaky? Nadia couldn't believe that Nate had used that word to describe their situation. What planet was he on?! She decided to wait two weeks before making any plans. There were always the options of bunking at her house with sleeping bags and staying at a motel. She just didn't want to deal with the problem; it was hard enough trying to keep everyone from asking questions.

Carrie and Kassie kept everyone entertained and busy at the farm. Arrangements had been made to have two high school girls help Ray and Mary babysit when the parents went to Minneapolis for the baseball games.

Nadia headed back to the Cities. She spent one entire morning at the University talking to her advisor about getting a doctorate in Psychology. They checked the availability of the courses she needed, and Nadia signed up for a full load for the Fall Semester. In the afternoon she went to the bank to discuss her financial situation. She was encouraged to buy bonds, which the financial advisor explained would earn her money more interest than just leaving it in a savings account, but Nadia refused to okay any change. "Keep everything the way it is," she told the advisor.

Nadia went home, plugged in her new phone and was delighted to discover that it worked instantly. She called home and gave Ray her new number. She also called Sal and Sandy and left a message. Her list of things to do was getting smaller. The next item was to go to a furniture store and buy some furniture for her apartment. While she waited for the men to deliver the furniture, she make a quick trip to Target where she actually had fun picking out rugs, dishes, towels and anything else that she needed to make her apartment feel like home.

At six o'clock, she joined the clan at the Lake Street Mission for dinner. It was a festive occasion, celebrating the many families who had relied on "My Way" to find jobs and had now moved into their own living quarters.

Nadia took in the inner city baseball playoffs, which she found to be fun and entertaining. She loved the little Mites the most. They took their games so seriously. It was also fun to watch the improvement that took place as the players moved up the levels. Sal coached a superb team of 15 and 16 year olds; they hadn't lost a game all summer. Sandy was their head cheerleader and had made sure that every parent, uncle, aunt, sister, brother and grandparent at the games was decked out in a new red t-shirt. Nadia was grateful for all of the businesses that sponsored the inner city baseball teams and made team shirts possible.

Nate and Nadia also sponsored a team in this older age group. Since Nate was usually away, Nadia attended most of the games alone. The championship game for their team was on a Sunday afternoon when Nate was gone, so Nadia had to coach. It turned out that their team, "Nate's Hawks", was playing "Sal's Angels" for the championship.

Just when the game was about to begin there was a commotion at the north end entrance. Nadia found herself praying, "Please, no gang battle today." When she opened her eyes, she could see that the cause of the excitement was making his way to the diamond.

"Hey, Nate, what are you doing here? Your appearance should be worth at least two extra runs."

"Hi, Farm Girl, I was afraid I wasn't going to make the championship game. We got in an hour ago. I didn't waste a minute—left the pickup at the airport and grabbed a cab."

They hadn't spoken to one another all week. Conversation now was a little awkward, but they managed to put aside their personal issues. Despite Sal's competitive zeal, one could see on his face how happy he was to have Nate coaching the opposing team, instead of Nadia. He shook Nate's hand. "Good luck, Big Guy. You're going to need it."

The game was even more exciting than the anticipation. After five innings it was 6-6. The scoreboard flashed 9-9 after nine innings, and the two teams were still battling after 16 innings. The coaches and umpire called a time out. After a few minutes, they declared that the league would have double champions. There wasn't one player or fan who was disappointed, since every one of these young men deserved to be a champion. Trophies couldn't be handed out until they could have a second one made, but no one seemed to care. Hundreds of players and fans enjoyed a meal of brats, hamburgers, potato salad and ice cream floats, all provided by Sandy.

As Nadia was walking to her car, Nate approached her. "Could I come over and see your new pad?"

"Sure, it'll take all of two minutes to give you the grand tour though."

It didn't take Nate long to make an assessment. "It's nice and homey. Nadia, I was wrong, very wrong. I knew that the second those words came out of my mouth. My teammates, family and friends are furious with me. They called me selfish, stupid and childish and other choice words. I hate to admit that I don't want to share you with anyone, but it's the truth. I'm gone so much that when I am home I want you to be there. But, I need you, Nadia, so I'll be happy with what I can have."

They visited and decided that a run would be good for both of them. Nate didn't ask to come in when they finished their run. "I have to go out of town tomorrow morning. We have a four-game road trip. I'm going to try and talk Kevin into staying at the house for the games though. I know that you guys have a lot planned but maybe I could take you all out to dinner on Saturday night. They opened a new sports bar just down the road from our house; Bert and a couple of other guys went there last weekend."

Nadia wasn't about to let him down easily. "You can see what Kevin and the rest want to do."

Her family arrived late Thursday night. It was well after midnight before they settled down. The floor of Nadia's apartment was one solid bed. There wasn't any place to walk around, so once a person got in bed, he had to stay there. Morning showers were the worst; each person got only fifteen minutes in the bathroom.

Their first stop the next morning was the North Side Mission for breakfast. Nadia's family was a big supporter of this mission and they wanted to see for themselves how their support helped. They were not disappointed. As they entered the building, bright smiling faces greeted them. Nadia made some introductions and then the five of them made their way through the breakfast line. They enjoyed pancakes, sausages, and orange juice. People kept coming and going. Some were on their way to jobs; others were in a hurry to go nowhere. It was the small children who captured everyone's hearts. They seemed to crave attention and asked a lot of questions: "Do you want to see my new shoes and socks?" "Do you know why I'm here—because my Mom got a job." The chatter was continuous. The Olsons stayed until the last person had been served. As they left, they promised to continue to help, both financially and spiritually.

They drove to Nate's house, a decision that wasn't made by Nadia. She was totally outnumbered. She cautioned everyone to be quiet because she didn't want to wake Nate, thinking that he would still be sleeping. She was wrong. Nate was up and had a pot of coffee ready. He had even made a trip to the bagel shop.

"It's good to see all of you. I didn't know what time you'd be here or if you'd even come over. Thanks for including me. What are you going to do today?"

Everyone started talking at once. They finally decided to rent bikes and have a picnic lunch at Lake Calhoun. At five o'clock, when everyone had eaten, they dropped Nate off at the stadium and headed home to get ready for the game.

On the way back to the stadium, the conversation was rapid and to the point. Kevin was the first to speak. "You two, why do you make each other's life so miserable? You know you'll get back together again. Too bad you're both so bullheaded."

Tony laughed. "Your sister comes by that stubbornness quite naturally."

Kevin tried to ignore the comment, but he had to add, "Yeah, I guess we are kind of the same."

Tony said, "Well, I wouldn't have said anything except that Ginny also fits that description."

Nadia put up her hand. "Okay, this conversation is going to end."

"Right." Kevin looked at her. "Just don't let the small stuff ruin this relationship for good."

She nodded. "Now, let's go have a good time."

Part 7

And they did. They were treated to a grand slam, two double plays, and great pitching. After the game they were invited to join eight other players and their wives. Nadia enjoyed spending time with the women; she learned a lot about being married to a baseball player. She realized how much the wives cherished the little time they had with their husbands during the season. Marion, a wife of one of the shortstops, was especially willing to share information. "I do everything when Chris is gone—doctor and dentist appointments for the kids, grocery shopping, oil changes, bill playing—so when he's home, we can spend every minute together as a family. The kids miss him, especially Jack, but the older boys realize that this is their Dad's job. Winter is heaven on earth. Nadia, we all talk about you and Nate. Everyone thinks that you should marry him."

"Don't you ever worry about your husband being unfaithful?"

"No," was the response from everyone present.

Later when they were driving home, Nadia looked at Nate. "Let's get married on February 12th. It's a Saturday, my birthday, and it would be our anniversary. You'd never forget all of the important occasions in our lives."

Nate pulled over to the emergency lane, slammed on the brakes and simply said, "Yes, let's do it!"

Kevin pulled up behind them and jumped out of the car, not knowing what to expect. "Will you be my best man?" Nate yelled out the window.

Kevin laughed, "It's about time. Get this bucket of bolts moving before we both get ticketed."

There was celebrating to do when they got home. Nadia had no idea how and when the guys got to bed. The women made plans to go shopping in the morning.

Nadia called home to tell Ray and Mary the news and bask in their excitement. Mary said that the babies were fine, and to tell Katie and Ginny that they had sent the sitters home last night. Nadia could hear Ray in the background, "Sure hope you don't change your mind after a couple of days!"

Nadia then called Jackie who yelled into the phone, "Yes, another prayer answered! Yours will be the wedding of the century."

"No, actually, it's just going to be our families and Sal and Sandy. We're getting married in the Bahamas."

"Perfect, but what about all your friends."

"Haven't thought that far ahead."

"Well, congratulations! I have to call John." Nadia could sense Jackie's joy across the miles.

The three women shopped for four hours. They returned to the house to find the men sitting on the deck with glasses of ice water. "How are your heads," Katie asked?

"Getting better every minute," retorted Kevin. "I'm not going to even asked how much money you women spent. My head couldn't withstand the slap."

After Nate left for the game, everyone took a long nap, a decision that made them have to race to get to the game on time. They were standing in line when Nadia heard a familiar voice, "Congratulations, Farm Girl!"

Nadia whipped around so quickly it felt as if her neck snapped. She ran over to Sal and Sandy. "What in the world are you two doing here?"

Sal said, "Nate called us in Florida and said he could get two tickets and he'd love to have us come and celebrate with everyone. We got a flight here but have no idea when we'll fly home. Every flight is booked for Monday. But who cares? Tuesday, Wednesday—we can catch up whenever we get home."

The Minnesota Twins were a joy to watch, and the fans showed their appreciation for the great entertainment. Nate hit his third grand slam of the year. It was the bottom of the ninth, 6-4 in favor of the Orioles, and the ball was gone! One of the huge screen replays flashed as he ran the bases. The crowd went wild.

The Olsons stayed in their seats until the crowd dispersed and Nate joined them. The evening was fun—good food and great company. They partied but not as extensively as the night before, since everyone was planning on playing golf the next morning.

Katie and Ginny called home to find out how their babies were doing. Mary answered the phone and told them that they couldn't talk long or they'd be late for church. "But," she said, "I wish that you girls wouldn't worry so much. The babies are fine. You know, Dad and I did a pretty good job taking care of you, and we haven't lost the touch."

On the golf course, it was Ginny, Tony, Nate and Nadia pitted against Jackie, John, Kevin and Katie. They played nine holes, stopped for a sandwich and finished the game. The score wasn't as lopsided as Nadia thought it would be.

They spent part of the evening grilling steaks and enjoying the hot tub. The other part was spent working on a schedule for Nate and Nadia's house on the farm. Kevin had sold Nate a couple of acres, just enough land for a house that already had its outside walls and roof. The cement had been poured for the sidewalks, patio and driveway, and the carpenters were scheduled to build the partitions in the next couple of days. Nate was hoping that, by the middle of October, the bathrooms and kitchen plumbing plus all of the electrical work would be completed. He had hired Kevin and Tony to do much of the inside work. They were fine with this arrangement as long as a carpenter would be there, supervising their work.

It was a beautiful home, by anyone's standards. There were five bedrooms, six bathrooms, an indoor pool, sauna, recreation room and movie theater. Nate was adamant that he would build only one home in his lifetime, and these blueprints had been in the making for years. Kevin asked him if this was also Nadia's idea of a dream home.

Nate smiled, "I wouldn't think of not checking with her. I've asked her for her input, and she's made some changes in my plans, believe me."

Nadia loved the house, and she told that to Nate. She thought it was huge, but was sure that she could give it a lived-in look when it was finished. Best of all, it was close to her family.

Nadia's life was pretty carefree. As soon as her classes were over for the day, she would check in at the missions to make sure that things were going okay.

The Twins won the pennant and went on to compete for the World Series title. Tony, Ginny, and Katie used their vacation days to join Nadia for the final game with the Mets in New York City. The anticipation had everyone on pins and needles. Neither team had won a game without extra innings during the season.

The final game of the series turned out to be no different from all the others. It was a perfect pitcher match-up; no runs had been scored in the first nine innings. In the bottom of the eleventh, though, a little known Twins player hit a home run, and the game was over. The Twins fans were greatly outnumbered, but you would never know that, given the cheering of those who were in attendance. Two World Series wins in three years—hard to beat that claim!

As quickly as the celebrations began, so did the rumors. Everyone was speculating on whether Nate would play another year. He wanted to lay the rumors to rest, but couldn't decide what to do. He was closing in on his 30th birthday. Baseball had treated him well, and, while he would rather play ball than do most things in life, there were also alternatives that sounded good to him. And then there was Nadia who had two more years of graduate school. It seemed reasonable that he should continue playing until she finished.

"What should I do, Farm Girl? I could go out in a blaze of glory or I could stick around another year for a third World Series title. I don't know. I guess we'll just put the subject on the back burner for a while. We have Jackie and John's wedding, our own wedding and a house to finish. Think about it though." The subject didn't come up for a couple of months, but everyone who knew Nate could tell that the decision was rolling around in his mind.

Jackie and John's wedding was glamorous—a New York wedding in Minneapolis! People commented on the diversity of the wedding party. Take John's groomsmen, for example: an African-American and a Hispanic friend, his two brothers-in-law and, of course, Nate. Nadia thought that maybe in a large city this wedding composition wouldn't have attracted so much attention, but in a small town in northern Minnesota, it was definitely a topic of conversation.

Mr. and Mrs. Patton spent five days with the Olson family. They had never spent any time on a farm before, never rode on four-wheelers, and never left doors unlocked or keys in their car. When they were leaving, John's father said, "It was a beautiful wedding and a wonderful vacation, Ray and Mary. I hope you won't mind if we visit you again some time."

Mary smiled, "We truly enjoyed having you. Maybe you could come back when the fishing is good. There's no better meal than the walleye we catch up here." After they left, she brought out the family calendar and wrote "Patton visit" on the June page.

Nadia and Nate, along with the Olsons, spent the Christmas holidays with Nate's family and, of course, Sal and Sandy. Nadia thought about how wonderful it was to have everyone together.

Christmas that year was made even more special than usual because Jackie announced that she was pregnant, and her baby was due in August. The Olsons received the news with characteristic enthusiasm: What could possibly be better than another new baby in the family?! Nadia found herself thinking ahead to the day when she and Nate would be making a similar announcement.

Minneapolis had been hit hard by the economic downturn, and that was no more evident than at the missions, which were filled to capacity. People had lost their jobs and were relying more than ever on food banks and clothes drop-offs. The Olson family didn't let the North Side Mission down. They spent two hours there one day, interacting with people and playing with the children. At one point, Nadia found Ray on the floor, putting together a farm of Lincoln Logs with four small boys. As he got up to join the rest he said, "This is what Christmas is all about, my friends. We have so much; they have so little. It sure feels good to help out a little."

Nate and Nadia few to the Bahamas to make final wedding plans and enjoy the warm temperatures. The day before New Year's Eve they flew back to Minnesota where it was a cool twenty below zero. Nadia shivered. "Tell me again why I want to live here for the rest of my life?"

Nate smiled, "Maybe we are nuts. You're positive that this is what you want, aren't you?"

"Never been more sure of anything in my life except my love for you."

Their house was coming along nicely. The ceilings had been textured, walls painted, tile laid and carpet installed. Nadia could hardly contain her excitement.

When they went shopping for furniture Nadia said, "This reminds me of when I was a little girl and Dad would give me a dollar to spend on anything I wanted. I know I have a lot more money to spend now, but it's still fun."

They spent a lot more than a dollar in the next few days. Mr. Alex, the owner of the furniture store, must have thought he had died and gone to heaven! They bought every piece of furniture from him; if he didn't have it in the store, he ordered it for them.

Mary was thrilled with the progress of the house. "Now if we could just get Jackie and John closer to home, everything would be perfect."

Nadia put her arm around her mother. "Don't push it, Mom. Let's get our houses finished first."

The Twins offered Nate a phenomenal one-year contract. Nadia thought it was almost sinful that one man should be considered to be worth so much money. She guessed that his presence on and off the field must be priceless; at least that's the way it seemed. She knew that he was good at motivating his teammates to play one notch higher every game. Well, this money would make them even more financially set than they already were.

They decided not to sell their house in Minneapolis. It would be a great place for everyone to congregate when they came to the Cities.

Nadia kept busy with her college courses and contacts with "her people" at the various centers. Nate spent weeks at the farm—snowmobiling, fishing, and carpentering on Tony's house. He had been negotiating the price for four hundred acres that were for sale. On Thursday night he called Nadia to tell her that they were now proud land owners. "I made the big purchase this afternoon. Kevin and I are going to rent it until I retire from baseball, and then I'm going to take over."

"You're actually going to be a farmer?" Nadia couldn't get used to that idea, even though Nate was consistent in his determination to make it happen.

"Easy, Farm Girl. I can do anything I set my mind to. You should see me with a hammer. I think I even impressed my brothers-in-law! One more thing: I deposited a fair amount of money in Tony's and Kevin's accounts. They won't realize anything until they get their statements. If they say something to you, let them know it's what I've wanted to do for a couple of years. It really bothers me to see Katie and Ginny going to work at midnight and coming home in the morning, trying to keep up with the kids and the house."

"How much are you talking about?"

"Let's just put it this way. They won't have to worry very much about working. I feel good about this. I've been blessed all my life, and now it's time to help make the lives of the people I love a little easier."

"I really do love you, Nate."

"Not nearly as much as I love you. Got to go. Ray and Kevin are here. It's time to get some meat for the table, or should I say, fish for the table,"

"Don't forget about Mom."

"Yeah, right, as if I could forget about my angel on earth,"

Time went by quickly. Before they knew it, the Olsons were boarding planes for the Bahamas. Nadia and Nate were married on February 12th. A sandy beach replaced a wood floor; blue skies substituted for a cathedral ceiling; and the sun was their warmth. It was a beautiful ceremony. Nate and Nadia had written their own vows. Nadia couldn't help but think of all the years it took for this occasion to happen—the rocky roads that seemed to have pot holes in them too large to get through—but love prevailed. Kassie and Carrie and every adult in attendance were overjoyed when two of their favorite people finally tied the knot.

Right after the ceremony Nate made an announcement: "Tonight, my fine families, you are on your own. I just want to say that I feel sorry for the man or woman who knocks on our door or calls on our phones. You will see us whenever we decide to join you. Goodnight."

Nadia blushed; her face went from a glowing bronze to a deep crimson. "I love all of you. Thank you so much for making this the best day of my life." With that, Nate lifted her up and carried her into the hotel. It was documented that they did not reappear until two o'clock the next day.

The weekend went by quickly. They spent the time scuba diving, sailing, and enjoying sunsets and sunrises. The highlight was a delicious seafood meal prepared for them by a local man they had hired to give them the best taste of the Bahamas. On the last day they starting dreading the return trip to the land of frigid temperatures, not even to be consoled by the fact that the snocats were ready to ride and the fish waiting to be caught at home. Nadia couldn't help but think that people who took vacations such as this one often couldn't possibly appreciate them as much as her family who indulged so infrequently.

Nate and Nadia went to the house as husband and wife for the first time. It was exciting. They had sublet Nadia's apartment to a young couple who was expecting their first child; the small space would suit them well until the baby was born. Nate left for spring training and Nadia started classes.

The phone was ringing as Nadia walked into the house one afternoon. It was Tony. "Hey, Gin and I have this huge balance in our checking account. The bank refused to tell us where it came from, and I don't suppose you'd care to enlighten us?"

Nadia smiled into the phone. "It's fine. There's no mistake. You'll have to talk to Nate—you know, the guy who wants everyone in the world to be happy?"

"But this is unbelievable, even for Nate"

"Just enjoy it. He wants to make sure that Ginny and Katie can stay home with the kids. He did the same thing for Kevin."

"Wow! I knew he was financially set, but I guess I underestimated his wealth. I'll talk to Kevin, and then call Nate. Thanks."

A few minutes after Nadia hung up, the phone rang again. She loved hearing the familiar voice say, "Hi, Farm Girl. How are you?"

"Hi Nate. You'll be getting phone calls from Tony and Kevin. They just discovered their windfall and called me to see if I knew anything about it, as if they didn't."

"Well, I love those guys like brothers. Did Kevin tell you that we are going to be an aunt and uncle again?"

"Yes, he did. I'm happy for them and you know, Jackie's pregnant too. "

"Are we going to be parents soon?"

"Not to my knowledge. We've only been married a few weeks."

"Gee, and here I thought I was a real man."

Nadia laughed. "Go back to practice. You guys need all the practice you can get. Every team in the league will be on you like flies on sugar this season."

"Love you. See you in a few days."

Nadia was planning on going to Florida to be with Nate during spring break. She needed a respite from her classes which were intense, especially one that focused on research for reflective practice in counseling. She would definitely have to go to school one more year. It seemed as if it was becoming increasingly hard to concentrate these days. Married life required more time than just being a girlfriend, and the missions relied on her visits; they called when a few days passed and they hadn't seen her. Nadia was thankful that she was young and in good health.

The baseball season was in full swing. It was when Nadia found out that the Twins had a home series in early June that she learned she was pregnant. It was difficult keeping the secret from Nate until he got home. She wanted to call him immediately. Instead, the day before he was scheduled to arrive, she stopped at the flower shop and purchased pink and blue carnations. She wrote on a big piece of tag board, "Welcome home, Daddy" and then proceeded to make his favorite meal of mashed potatoes, corn, meatballs and gravy.

The garage door opened. Nate didn't get all the way into the kitchen before he noticed the sign and flowers.

"Wow! Yes, yes, yes! Thank you!

"I believe it took both of us to make this happen."

He held onto her. "We'll be the best parents ever. When are you due?"

"February 15th. Can you imagine how busy you'll be every year for those three days and all the money you'll have to spend on our anniversary, birthdays and Valentine's Day?"

Nate was ebullient. "Can I call a few people before we sit down for dinner or have you already told everyone?"

"Not a soul. I waited for you."

Nate called everyone he knew and even some he didn't know well! It was 8:30 before they sat down to eat.

Nadia had a bad case of morning sickness for the first three months. She ate so many Saltine crackers that Nate considered buying stock in the company. After the first trimester they went to the doctor together and Nadia had an ultrasound, which revealed a shocking surprise: twins!

Nate laughed, "I can't believe I was that good."

Nadia failed to see the humor of his remark at that point. Outside of the doctor's office, Nate looked at her and said, "You're so quiet, Farm Girl."

"I'm scared."

"Thousands of women have multiple births every year. Don't worry."

They spent the entire evening in quiet conversation and in reading all of the pamphlets and books the doctor had given them.

Nadia couldn't understand the feelings she was having. She decided that she was probably depressed, but why would she be depressed? This was supposed to be the good trimester—a happy, joyous time. Nothing that she had studied in her psychology classes could explain depression after the first trimester and before postpartum.

The next few days dragged by. Between crying and staring out the window, Nadia forced herself to go to her classes and the missions. She counted on her friends at the missions to change her mood. Nate tried to be patient, but it was hard for him to understand what was going on. When Nadia took him to the airport on Friday morning, she assured him that she would go to the doctor to find out what was wrong with her.

At the doctor's office later in the day, everyone congratulated Nadia. She listened as Dr. Peterson talked to her about depression. He couldn't give her an exact diagnosis, but he did give her a prescription with the assurance that it wouldn't harm the babies.

"The best advice I can give you, Nadia, is to go home to the farm. Spend some time there—playing golf, being around your nieces, and helping your mother. Enjoy the things that make you happy. You can fight this, Nadia, don't let it drown you."

Nadia left his office, called Nate, and drove home to the farm.

Mary greeted her at the door. "Well, hello Mommy. I've got some vegetable soup with dumplings on the stove for you. Dad and I waited to have supper."

Two bowls of soup later they got into the car and drove to Kevin's. It was absolutely the best medicine. Kassie and Carrie were going full throttle and Ginny and Katie were exhausted. Nadia took all of this in, and mused, "How in the world am I ever going to handle two of them by myself?"

"You won't have to, Sis," said Ginny. "Your husband will be right there to help you. Life does have a way of changing when children enter the equation, but the changes are wonderful. Every day, these two do something they haven't done before and say something they've never said before. It's great!"

Katie nodded. "You look good, Nadia. In fact, I don't think you've ever looked so good."

They visited for hours. The little girls talked Ray into being the conductor for their human train. Tony took up the rear. Nate called while they were in full play mode. He asked to talk to Kevin.

"Take good care of her, Kevin, and keep her there until I get home."

"You got it, Boss." Kevin gave Nadia the message.

The next morning, Nadia went to her own farm house. It was a beautiful and inviting sight. Even though she hadn't spent much time there, Mary and Ray had made sure that flowers and shrubs had been planted and the grass mowed, trimmed and watered. The whole scene was perfect.

Nadia made her way into the nursery. It was empty and quiet now, but in a few months it would be anything but. She called the girls and invited them for a late afternoon lunch. Then she made a list of groceries that were needed for a chicken salad. Nate called just as she was about to leave for the grocery store. He couldn't help but hear the excitement in Nadia's voice.

"Nate, would it be all right with you if I forgo college for a while and stay here? I feel like my old self. I have energy; I laugh; and I want to get the nursery ready. The whole bunch of us have picked games we want to come and watch. I talked to your sister and she's going to meet us for the Tampa Bay series. I even went for a long walk with Buford. Is it okay if I spend a lot of money at the grocery store? I'd like to get the cupboards stocked with the necessities."

"Whoa, slow down there, Farm Girl, take a breath. You can do anything you want except hustle men. Oh yeah, in your condition I don't have to worry about that." They both laughed.

A back seat, a trunk full of groceries and $305.00 later, she was on her way home. The ingredients for the chicken salad had been placed in a separate bag so she put the chicken breasts in the oven even before she started carrying the dozens of bags inside.

She heard a familiar voice. "We thought you'd need a little help getting these in the house."

"Dad and Kevin, am I ever glad to see you!"

It took eight trips to get everything in from the car. The entire kitchen floor was carpeted with bags. Ray said, "We were on our way to rake and bale and wanted to see how you were doing. Now that I know how you're doing, I'm glad we stopped by."

Nadia laughed. "Seriously, sometimes I think you have ESP."

Kevin walked over to Nadia. "We forgot water. Do you have a big jug we can fill up?"

Nadia filled a jug up with ice and water, put a couple of glasses in a bag, and sent her Dad and brother on their way. She thought about how much she enjoyed being a homemaker—here in her house, with people who needed little things, such as a jug of water.

The four ladies enjoyed a leisurely luncheon on the deck while the two little girls entertained themselves on Auntie's playground. After eating, Katie told them that she was a little uncomfortable and thought that tonight might be the big night. She was right. True to her instincts, Christian was born that night. He came into the world with a bang, five minutes after they arrived at the hospital. He had a full head of dark brown hair. Where did that hair come from in a family of blondes, Nadia wondered.

Conner Anthony made his appearance nine days later: no hair, 21 inches long and a little over seven pounds. The delivery took a lot longer than that of his cousin—fourteen hours longer! When it was over, Ginny announced that she was having no more children—period.

Nadia hoped she would be blessed with a "Christian" delivery.

She and Nate cherished their time together. Dozens of times he repeated the same statement: "I wish I had never signed another contract. My heart just isn't into baseball anymore. I try to put on a happy face whenever I'm with the team, but I'm sure they all can see right through it."

Nadia took him by the shoulders. "You have a few months left. Give it your all. You're being paid big bucks for your contribution, and you'd better make the team feel as if you're worth every penny."

Part 8

Life on the farm was anything but quiet. Haying, harvesting, gardening, mowing and babies kept the Olsons busy. Everyone was looking forward to meeting Elizabeth Patton who had been born on August 7th. Jackie planned to introduce Libby to the family in a few days and would spend two weeks on the farm. John had accepted a position with Thompson, Thompson and Bearle, a law firm in Minneapolis, so he would be looking for a house while Jackie was at the farm.

It seemed as though someone was always making a trip to Minneapolis. The men would work like dogs, get things caught up and then take off for the Cities for a baseball game or two. The Twins had won the American League pennant and were bound for the World Series to play the Yankees again. It was good to see Nate pumped up.

Nadia moved back to the Minneapolis house for a couple of weeks so that she would be close to the action. She was getting bigger by the day but felt good most of the time. When her family came down for some home games, they all stayed at her house. Nate, as usual, was 'locked up' with the team in a motel, so he couldn't spend much time with them.

Nadia visited the food banks, missions and her "adopted families". She and John spent hours setting up account funds for each location. They interviewed people until they were able to hire four individuals they felt would work together to make sure everyone's needs would be met. The pay wasn't great, but the benefits were fantastic—smiles, hugs and gratitude when people received warm meals, new clothes and assistance in finding a job.

Another World Series championship wasn't in the cards for the Twins. They lost to the Yankees in five games. The Olsons were all in New York for the final game. Ray and Mary stayed back in Minneapolis to babysit with the help of two high school girls. This time they accepted help. Even Mary, the superwomen, realized that five children under the age of three would be a bit much for her and Ray. Besides, it wasn't hard to find two willing high school girls who needed money.

The Olsons had gone from the "fab five" to the "energized eight." They spent a couple of extra days in New York, visiting John's parents and playing the role of tourists. They actually reminded themselves of the Energizer Bunnies—kept going and going until they fell into bed at night. Nadia got exhausted but refused to stay back and miss anything.

Nate went back to the farm with them. Nadia felt warm and secure inside. For some reason she knew at that moment that they would be together forever, and nothing or no one would be able to separate them. She came close to hitting him, though, when he left the house after being there for less than an hour. "Kevin needs me to help him haul hay."

"Absolutely, he's never done that alone before." Nadia couldn't keep the sarcasm out of her voice, but she was smiling inside.

Out the door he went, happy as a lark. Nadia actually started to believe that Nate had been born to be a farmer.

Jackie, John and Libby agreed to live in Nadia and Nate's house for the time being. It was comforting to know that someone would be there to care for everything. Jackie and John were close to buying a house that Jackie loved. The price was right; in fact, it was a steal, something that made John nervous since he didn't want to be known as a thief.

Thanksgiving was celebrated at Ginny and Tony's. They made plans to spend Christmas at Kevin and Katie's, Easter at Jackie and John's, and the Fourth of July at Nate and Nadia's. "And what's going to be celebrated at Ray and Mary's?" asked Mary.

Nadia put her arm around her mother. "Don't worry, Mom. There'll still be plenty of family visits at the Olson homestead. At some point you'll be wishing that it was time we all stayed home."

Mary shook her head. "I doubt that will ever happen."

Nate and Nadia quickly became acclimated to country living. Mary was determined that she would teach all of the women to quilt, so on Tuesday afternoons they would gather in the basement to work on four sewing machines set up on a huge table. Nadia couldn't believe that there would be enough material to go around, but there was. Mary insisted that everyone do her best. Nadia and Katie were naturals while Ginny—well, let's just say that Ginny enjoyed the visiting and baking. No one minded that she didn't take to quilting, though, since they relished her baked goods. `

There was only one rule at Grandma and Grandpa's house when everyone—from the youngest to the oldest—got together: parents changed their kids' diapers and heated the bottles. Grandpa and Grandma were allowed to rock and feed the little ones. Nadia couldn't help but notice how happy Mary and Ray seemed when their house was rocking with activity and excitement.

Minnesota experienced a true arctic winter that year—48 inches of snow on the ground by January 1st which, of course, made snocatting, skiing, ice fishing, and sledding the best. For eight days the thermometer never went above the twenty below line. With the wind chill, it felt as if it were forty below much of the time. School was even cancelled on a couple of days.

On the ninth day, the temperature climbed to two below, and everyone celebrated the "summer-like" weather. It must have been a significant change because even the cattle started moving around again.

Nadia moved as little as possible during those days. She was two weeks away from her due date—big as a house, slow-moving, bad temperament, and a tendency to weep at the smallest suggestion of criticism. Nate teased her, "I'm going to move in with Ray and Mary if those two little ones don't come soon."

February 12th was a beautiful day: light snow, no wind, and 25 degrees above zero. Katie was preparing a birthday dinner for everyone. John, Jackie and Libby were home for the weekend. Suddenly, Nadia panicked, "Nate, my water broke. We've got to go!"

Nate grabbed the suitcase. "Oh shit, what if we don't make it to the hospital."

Nadia stuffed herself in the car and Nate climbed in on the driver's side. Twenty miles wasn't a long trip in normal times, but today it seemed to take hours. "You'd better speed it up," Nadia warned.

Moments after they pulled into the emergency parking garage, Nadia was on a stretcher. Nine minutes later, Hunter Ray and Hannah Mary were born. They were identical in weight and height: six pounds, five ounces and 20 inches long. Nadia had never seen such perfect babies.

Nate was a wreck; Nadia needed to sleep; and the babies wanted to eat. Everyone got his wish, thanks to the efficiency of the hospital staff. The entire family had arrived, including Sal and Sandy and Nate's parents. They took turns congratulating Nadia and then were told they had to leave. All Nadia wanted to do was sleep. The nurses asked her if she'd like to feed one of the twins, but she said that Nate could do it. Finally, after twenty hours of sleep, she got up, took a shower, did her hair, put on a little makeup and was ready to take on the role of being a mother.

Nate and Nadia celebrated Valentine's Day in the hospital. Red roses decorated not only Nadia's room, but the nurses' station and the hallway also. The floral shop owner thought Nate was joking when he ordered thirty dozen roses.

On February 15th, all three were discharged from the hospital. Nadia knew that the fun was just now beginning. With the exception of John and Tony who had to go back to work, everyone pitched in to help. They had to make a schedule so that all who wanted to help would get a chance to feed, change and rock the babies.

Nadia took advantage of the help. "Nate, what are we going to do when everyone goes home?"

"Be sleep deprived, I guess."

Nadia and Nate developed a routine with Hunter and Hannah that got them through the next few weeks. They both enjoyed taking care of the babies and ensuring their well-being.

Mary was their saving grace. She would magically show up when most needed—to rock the babies to sleep and then slip into the kitchen and heat up a casserole she had prepared for dinner.

Spring finally arrived and was very welcome after the harsh winter. Hannah and Hunter were baptized on May 15th. They each had double sets of godparents because Nadia and Nate couldn't choose among all of the siblings. They wanted everyone to be included in the spiritual care of their children.

The Olsons and Sal and Sandy vacationed in northern Minnesota that summer. Nadia didn't know how Kevin found the time in his busy schedule, but he planned a fishing trip, golf outings, picnics and boating around the islands in the Northwest Angle. It was, as usual, a great time.

Time flew by. Nate and Nadia brought the kids to a Twins game in July. They had an opportunity to visit with players and their families. They visited all of the missions where everything was going well and success stories abounded. They also visited Nadia's advisor at the University. Nadia hadn't given up on her goal of getting doctorate, and she told her advisor that she wanted to start taking classes again. Her advisor, however, had some advice for her: "Give yourself a little more time with the children, Nadia. There's no doubt in my mind that you will reach your goal."

The Snowy family enjoyed every day at the farm. The twins loved going on walks to Grandpa and Grandma's and to their cousins' houses. Nate really got into farming. He would come home after a day in the field, looking like a man who felt satisfied about his choice of careers.

Nate and Nadia sold their house in Minneapolis and bought a condo—no yard work or maintenance. They celebrated Thanksgiving and drew names for Christmas. They selected the charity that would receive a special monetary gift from the Olson family. Once again, they felt happy and thankful to be so blessed.

Nate rented a house in Florida for January, February and March. Everyone came down and vacationed at some point. One family would leave and the next would arrive. Nate spent some time in Minnesota ice fishing and snowmobiling but not Nadia and the twins who preferred sun, sand, and warm temperatures. Katie, Ginny, Jackie and their children also loved Florida. Ray and Mary, however, sought the colder climate of Norway where they rekindled friendships with family.

Kassie and Carrie started school. Nadia lived through the terrible twos and before she knew it, the twins turned four. She started working on her doctorate again and walked down the graduation aisle at the University of Minnesota one more time.

She realized that she probably would never use the degree in a professional sense, but it would serve her well in other ways.

Several retired Twins players organized an alumni game to be played before the regular Twins game against the White Sox. Invitations were sent out to all retired players. The RSVPs came in quickly; it was obvious that the Oldies would have no problem fielding a team. Nadia was excited because all proceeds would go to "My Way."

Before long all of the seats were sold out. In addition to purchasing a seat at the game, many people sent in checks for hundreds of dollars, and Nadia couldn't believe the wonderful generosity she was observing.

At 1:00 on Saturday afternoon, the umpire hollered "Batter up!" The crowd roared when the Oldies came out on the field. They roared even louder when Nate appeared. He was still considered a home town favorite.

The Twins were up 8-5 in the top of the eighth. Nate was coaching third base when the unthinkable happened: A line drive foul ball hit him on the side of his head. He fell to the ground and lay motionless. Gasps of silence filled the stadium and then there was complete silence. Kevin, Tom, and Nadia flew down the stairs and stood motionless as doctors from around the stadium appeared to help the ambulance drivers. The ambulance drive to the hospital was the longest ride Nadia had ever experienced. Two miles seemed like an eternity.

Family members filled the waiting room. Not a word was spoken; everyone was in shock. After hours of waiting, the doctor came into the room to deliver the somber news.

"Nate is in critical condition. He has bleeding and swelling on the brain. A surgeon we're flying in from Boston will do surgery as soon as he arrives. Right now that is all I can tell you." Nadia passed out. The doctor continued, "We will keep him sedated until the surgery is completed and we have a better understanding of the situation."

Players and their wives began arriving. The outside parking lot was beginning to look like a scene from a movie. Hundreds of people were milling around with no one saying anything, just like the family inside the hospital. Someone took the children to John and Jackie's. They didn't want to go and kept wailing, "We want Mommy and Daddy." The only person who had a calming effect on them was Mary. She and Ray went to the house and stayed with them.

Nate came through the surgery, but the prognosis was worse than they had been led to believe: the doctors had no way of knowing if the damage to the brain would be permanent.

Nadia spent every minute at the hospital. She was so thankful for loving family and friends. How could life change so drastically?

Everyone lived the next six months day by day. Kevin and Tony took care of everything at their farm home and John looked after the Minneapolis condo. Mary never left Nadia and the twins. Ray was steadfast in his belief that Nadia needed Mary more than he did at home.

Nadia tried her best to be strong but she found out that coping with the stress from having someone you love in a coma wasn't one of her strong points. But she knew that she had to be upbeat for the children.

Christmas that year was a difficult time. Everyone gave 100% to make the holiday happy and joyful for the kids. Nate still showed no improvement. The doctors encouraged the family in every way possible, but eventually that was a difficult task since there was never a change.

Hannah and Hunter celebrated their fifth birthday. Nadia enrolled them in kindergarten in the fall. It was good for them to go to school, since it distracted them from their father's situation. Every day they would bring home papers from school and, after Nadia had looked at them, she would place them in a container so someday their Daddy would have the opportunity to see them. They loved to spend weekends on the farm. Usually, Jackie and John would drive them the three hundred fifty miles on a Friday and come back on Sunday.

Nadia fell into a routine—drop the kids off at school and head for the hospital. One day, she visited with the nurses as usual, got a cup of coffee, and settled into her chair next to Nate's bed. She finished another chapter in the book she was reading to him and got up to go to the bathroom. She stood up and leaned down to give him a kiss, as she always did when she left the room. This time, Nate opened his eyes and said, "Hey, Farm Girl."

Nadia pushed the emergency button on his bed. The nurses came running into the room. Between sobs, Nadia cried, "Call the doctor. Nate just called me by name."

Nate was perplexed by all the activity in the room. He kept asking, "What's going on?"

The doctors sent Nadia out of the room. She took the opportunity to call her parents, his parents, Sal and Sandy, John, Kevin and Tony. Everyone said the same thing: "It's a miracle, Nadia!"

Nadia was asked to come back into the room. There she saw that Nate was carrying on a conversation with Dr. Zeroba. She heard him say, "I have to get out of here. There's so much work to be done on the farm and I have to help Nadia with the twins."

Of course, the doctors won that battle. They told Nate that he wouldn't be going anywhere for some time, not until they had completed a battery of tests, anyway.

News of Nate's recovery reached the newspapers and television. He received literally hundreds of cards and letters at the hospital, his home, and at the Twins office. Family members came from all over. Nate's parents flew in from Sioux Falls, a trip they had made countless times in the past months but for different reasons. This trip was filled with excitement and relief.

Nate's sister flew in from Colorado; Sal and Sandy from Florida; and, of course, his entire family was there.

Nate made a quick mental recovery; it was his physical recovery that took time. He wanted to jump out of bed and run out of the hospital, but he had to learn how to walk, stand and sit first. He was released two weeks to the day he came out of his coma and talked to Nadia. The first decision they made as a family was to stay in Minneapolis for a while. The twins were sad about that decision. They wanted to go home.

Nate continued to make progress while at home. He met with his doctors twice a week until they gave him the stamp of approval to go home. It amazed Nadia and everyone around him how quickly his life returned to normal.

Before leaving Minneapolis, Nate met with his banker to set up trust funds for Hunter and Hannah. He made sure that Nadia would be financially secure for the rest of her life if anything should happen to him. When those tasks were completed, they loaded the car and set out for home. It was extremely difficult to leave Jackie and John. They had been Nadia and Nate's lifeline and could be counted on in any situation.

On their way home, they made a quick stop at their pastor's house to thank him personally for his kindness and prayers. Just as they were backing out of his driveway, Nadia realized that the song playing on the radio was "On the Road Again" by Willie Nelson. For some reason, it made her feel hopeful. She looked at Nate. "We'll never look back—only ahead."

Excitement grew as they got closer to home. The children could hardly contain their enthusiasm. Hannah tapped Nadia on the shoulder, "Mom, can we bike over to Uncle Kevin's when we get home?"

Nate turned around and laughed, "You betcha, just make sure that you watch for cars and stay on your side of the road."

Hunter protested, "Dad, you don't have to worry about us. We're almost six years old." He stared out the window and spoke again, "Wow, look at all those balloons. There must be hundreds of them!"

Starting at the three mile corner, balloons and bows adorned every sign and tree until Nate turned into the driveway. A huge sign was swaying in the breeze: God Answers Prayers. Nadia sent another prayer of thanks upward. The twins didn't have to bike anywhere because everyone was there. Hunter jumped out of the car. "I've never seen so many balloons in my life. Where did you get them? Grandpa, who blew them all up? Uncle Kevin and Uncle Tony, can we have rides on the four wheelers?"

Hannah was jumping up and down. "Grandma, will you make me some clothes for my baby? She only has one dress?"

Cassie ran over to them. "Let's all of us kids build a fort."

The adults stood back and allowed the cousins to reconnect. Within minutes they were deep into their play. All of a sudden, Hannah left the group and ran to Nate. "Daddy, you have to be careful so nothing hits you." Then she was off to join the other children.

Ray looked at Nadia, "You two will probably never get those kids to leave this yard."

While everyone was eating, Nate started thanking people and was cut off by Tony. "Stop right now! You would have done the same things if anything would have happened to one of us."

A child's voice cut in. "Grandpa, will you help us build a tree house? We know that if you help, then our Dads will help too."

That ended the visit. All four men jumped up and within minutes hammers were pounding, saws were buzzing, and a pickup left the yard only to return with more lumber. Nadia knew this wouldn't be any ordinary tree house. This would be the ultimate tree house. The children were so excited they incessantly asked questions without waiting for answers: "Grandma, will you sew the curtains? Mom, can we have the rug from our kitchen? Is it all right if we sleep in our new house tonight?"

For the next few days, all of the kids spent every waking moment in the backyard. They were voting to see who could sleep in the tree house when Nate intervened, "Listen, this tree house is for everyone. If you don't share, then Dad and your uncles will take it down."

Nate and Nadia enjoyed the beautiful summer. The activity level was at a constant ten. Mary sewed the curtains and made many dresses for Hannah's doll. Nate farmed from morning to night. He and Kevin purchased another four hundred acres and hired another full time hand. They became increasingly protective of Ray, not allowing him to work hard. "Relax," they would say, "enjoy all of the grandkids and help Mary with the garden." They never had to tell him twice. He listened and took their advice.

Jackie and Libby spent all of August on the farm. They split their time evenly among the three families. Sal and Sandy and Tom and Gloria made frequent visits, loving the opportunity to be with everyone and fish for hours at a time.

Nadia tried to convince Nate to go watch a few Twins games. "Not yet," he always said and went on to another conversation. He continued to have regular checkups with Dr. Anderson and his doctor at University Hospital.

Hunter, Hannah, and the cousins wore sad faces when they had to begin the school year. "Why can't we just stay home and play?"

"We've answered that question dozens of times. Now, off to school and behave yourselves." Nadia gave them both a gentle shove out the door. Then she was off to one of her many charities with which she insisted on maintaining contact.

Nadia and Nate purchased a home on the Outer Banks in North Carolina. It was a huge house—eight bedrooms, two lofts, a formal dining room, playroom and a kitchen that would feed thousands! The empty lot on one side of the house was also a selling factor. The Olsons needed a lot of room, because when they visited, they usually arrived in busloads. Nate loved it when the house was full, and realized that his fears of the house not being used were totally groundless. That would never happen—not with this family!

Nate was involved in baseball at all levels. He coached Hunter's team every year. And Nadia was just as happy to share her expertise with young golfers, especially those on the high school girls' team.

The days and evenings continued to be activity-filled and busy. The older the children got, the more baseball and golf outings Nadia and Nate attended. They didn't have just their own children, but every child in the neighborhood wanted to be at the Snowy house.

John and Jackie moved to northern Minnesota after their son Jack was born. He was a huge addition to the family—literally—weighing in at ten pounds, 14 ounces. No wonder Jackie called herself "the Goodyear blimp" the last two months of her pregnancy. Ray and Mary knew that Jack would be the last grandchild they would have to spoil—they and everyone else in the family.

John started his own hometown practice; he and Jackie had decided to raise their children in a small town. Jackie was elated when their house in Minneapolis sold and they started building their new home.

Nadia and Nate enjoyed every day, but it was the evenings they looked forward to the most. Hunter and Hannah would be sleeping, the dishes washed, and Nadia and Nate would cozy up on the deck when weather permitted or on the couch in the family room. They always managed a few precious minutes together, just the two of them. During some evenings, very few words were spoken—the exchange of a kiss or a glance was sufficient communication. Nadia was reminded during those moments of how much she loved Nate—always had and always would. Life was very good.

The years rolled on, marked by both happy and sad events. One of the most devastating for the Olsons was the accident that killed Sal and Sandy. The head-on collision with a semi in Florida was almost too much for Nadia to think about. She kept wondering where she would be today if it hadn't been for her chance encounter with Sal and Sandy at the Twins baseball game so long ago. They were loving and generous people.

Nadia was also grateful for the continued health of both her and Nate's parents. Every day they felt blessed when they could enjoy visits and phone calls with them.

Hunter was a chip off the old block. Baseball was his passion and his enthusiasm rubbed off on all his cousins. Three years in a row his high school baseball team went to State, with Nate as the coach.

While Nate coached baseball, Nadia worked with the girls' golf team. She was willing to hold clinics for anyone interested in learning the game.

Kassie and Carrie graduated and enrolled at the University of Minnesota, one majoring in social work and the other in business. Hunter and Hannah, Christian, Connor and Libby were close behind them. The twins' senior year was exciting and sad at the same time. Nate and Nadia talked a lot about how their lives were about to change.

One night when they were sitting on the porch, Nate turned to Nadia, "Just think, Farm Girl, you'll get to spend every minute with me now."

Nadia smiled, "I can't think of anyone in the world I'd rather spend my life with."

A graduation present to remember! This was how the twins explained their graduation gift from Nate and Nadia. Nate had worked for hours during the last months to arrange a vacation of a lifetime. Every member of both families went on a two-month vacation to Europe and the Scandinavian countries. They did and saw everything in all of the countries—days filled with tourist activities and nights marked by deep sleep. The highlight of the trip was Paris, where Nate and Nadia renewed their wedding vows. During dinner at a beautiful Parisian restaurant, Nate gave a speech that left everyone laughing and crying at the same time.

"Never in my lifetime did I think I could love so many people, but I do. I love all of you. I hope that you will always take good care of each other and never take a single day for granted. And you young people, reach for the stars. You can achieve whatever you think is important as long as you have faith in yourselves and in God. I love you, Farm Girl. Thank you for making almost every day of my life wonderful."

They flew home on Labor Day just in time for everyone to get back to work and school. Nate and Nadia fell into bed exhausted. Nadia awoke with a start the next morning, knowing before she even looked that Nate wasn't lying in bed with her. She ran to the living room and saw him sitting at the desk with his head resting on a file full of papers. She knew instantly that God had taken him home. Hysterical, she called Kevin who came over immediately. The next few days were a blur.

Nate Snowy passed away on September 4th, one day short of his 50th birthday. They say that a funeral brings closure to mourners. Nadia found that not to be true; in fact, the funeral only made her want Nate more. She couldn't believe that he was gone from her life.

One evening, she sat down with the twins to go over the papers in Nate's folder. "Nadia, Hannah, and Hunter, the three most precious people in my life . . . ." Nadia managed to finish reading the letter, which included details about Nate's health. He had received the news of the inoperable tumor that was growing in his brain. The doctors had given him six months to a year to live. Nadia realized that this explained his quick trips to Minneapolis and the frequent conversations with his banker. It also explained the desperation Nate felt in getting everyone he loved together one last time.

Nadia remained on the farm for the next four years and then moved back to Minneapolis. Hunter and Hannah graduated from college. Hunter signed his first major league contract with the Twins, while Hannah went on to play professional golf, with the promise that she "wanted to be the best woman golfer ever, next to my Mom."

Ray passed away in March of the following year. Mary was devastated and mourned his passing until she died six months later. The Olsons drew comfort from the knowledge that Mary and Ray would be together forever in a wonderful place. They also drew comfort from one another and tried harder than ever to live their lives filled with love and compassion for everyone they knew.

Nadia threw herself back into "My Way." She took pride in helping someone turn his life around—find a job, go to college, and enjoy success. She never remarried. When asked about that aspect of her life, she replied, "Not a chance. I met and married the love of my life. There could never be another man who could bring happiness into my life and into the lives of those I love the way Nate did."